THE DARK LIGHT YEARS

The Dark Light Years

BRIAN W. ALDISS

NEW ENGLISH LIBRARY

TIMES MIRROR

First published in Great Britain by Faber & Faber Ltd. in 1964
Second impression 1964
© 1964 by Brian W. Aldiss

∗

First Four Square edition February 1966
REISSUED IN THIS NEL EDITION MAY 1971
This new edition March 1975

∗

NEL Books are published by The New English Library Limited, from Barnard's Inn, Holborn, London, E.C.1. Made and printed in Great Britain by C. Nicholls & Company Ltd.

4500 23060

A few light years
with artificial flavouring
for
HARRY HARRISON
poet, philosopher, pacemaker, pieman

O dark dark dark. They all go into the dark,
The vacant interstellar spaces, the vacant into
  the vacant,
The captains, merchant bankers, eminent men
  of letters,
The generous patrons of art, the statesmen and
  the rulers. . . .

T. S. Eliot

CHAPTER ONE

On the ground, new blades of grass sprang up in chlorophyll coats. On the trees, tongues of green protruded from boughs and branches, wrapping them about – soon the place would look like an imbecile Earthchild's attempt to draw Christmas trees – as spring again set spur to the growing things in the southern hemisphere of Dapdrof.

Not that nature was more amiable on Dapdrof than elsewhere. Even as she sent the warmer winds over the southern hemisphere, she was sousing most of the northern in an ice-bearing monsoon.

Propped on G-crutches, old Aylmer Ainson stood at his door, scratching his scalp very leisurely and staring at the budding trees. Even the slenderest outmost twig shook very little, for all that a stiffish breeze blew.

This leaden effect was caused by gravity; twigs, like everything else on Dapdrof, weighed three times as much as they did on Earth. Ainson was long accustomed to the phenomenon. His body had grown round-shouldered and hollow-chested accustoming him to it. His brain had grown a little round-shouldered in the process.

Fortunately he was not afflicted with the craving to recapture the past that strikes down so many humans even before they reach middle age. The sight of infant green leaves woke in him only the vaguest nostalgia, roused in

7

him only the faintest recollection that his childhood had been passed among foliage more responsive to April's zephyrs – zephyrs, moreover, a hundred light years away. He was free to stand in the doorway and enjoy man's richest luxury, a blank mind.

Idly, he watched Quequo, the female utod, as she trod between her salad beds and under the ammp trees to launch her body into the bolstering mud. The ammp trees were evergreen, unlike the rest of the trees in Ainson's enclosure. Resting in the foliage on the crest of them were big four-winged white birds, which decided to take off as Ainson looked at them, fluttering up like immense butterflies and splashing their shadows across the house as they passed.

But the house was already splashed with their shadows. Obeying the urge to create a work of art that visited them perhaps only once in a century, Ainson's friends had broken the white of his walls with a scatterbrained scattering of silhouetted wings and bodies, urging upwards. The lively movement of this pattern seemed to make the low-eaved house rise against gravity; but that was appearance only, for this spring found the neoplastic rooftree sagging and the supporting walls considerably buckled at the knees.

This was the fortieth spring Ainson had seen flow across his patch of Dapdrof. Even the ripe stench from the middenstead now savoured only of home. As he breathed it in, his grorg or parasite-eater scratched his head for him; reaching up, Ainson returned the compliment and tickled the lizard-like creature's cranium. He guessed what the grorg really wanted, but at that hour, with only one of the suns up, it was too chilly to join Snok Snok Karn and Quequo Kifful with their grorgs for a wallow in the mire.

"I'm cold standing out here. I am going inside to lie down," he called to Snok Snok in the utodian tongue.

The young utod looked up and extended two of his

8

limbs in a sign of understanding. That was gratifying. Even after forty years' study, Ainson found the utodian language full of conundrums. He had not been sure that he had not said, "The stream is cold and I am going inside to cook it." Catching the right whistling inflected scream was not easy: he had only one sound orifice to Snok Snok's eight. He swung his crutches and went in.

"His speech is growing less distinct than it was," Quequo remarked. "We had difficulty enough teaching him to communicate. He is not an efficient mechanism, this manlegs. You may have noticed that he is moving more slowly than he did."

"I had noticed it, Mother. He complains about it himself. Increasingly he mentions this phenomenon he calls pain."

"It is difficult to exchange ideas with Earthlegs because their vocabularies are so limited and their voice range minimal, but I gather from what he was trying to tell me the other night that if he were a utod he would now be almost a thousand years old."

"Then we must expect he will soon evolve into the carrion stage."

"That, I take it, is what the fungus on his skull signified by changing to white."

This conversation was carried out in the utodian language, while Snok Snok lay back against the huge symmetrical bulk of his mother and soaked in the glorious ooze. Their grorgs climbed about them, licking and pouncing. The stench, encouraged by the sun's mild shine, was gorgeous. Their droppings, released in the thin mud, supplied valuable oils which seeped into their hides, making them soft.

Snok Snok Karn was already a large utod, a strapping offspring of the dominant species of the lumbering world of Dapdrof. He was in fact adult now, although still neuter: and in his mind's lazy eye he saw himself as a male for the next few decades anyhow. He could change sex when Dapdrof changed suns; for that event, the periodical entropic solar orbital disestablishment, Snok Snok was well prepared. Most of his lengthy childhood had been taken up with disciplines preparing him for this event. Quequo had been very good on disciplines and on mindsuckle; secluded from the world as the two of them were here with Manlegs Ainson, she had given them all of her massive and maternal concentration.

Languidly, he deretracted a limb, scooped up a mass of slime and mud, and walloped it over his chest. Then, re-collecting his manners, he hastily sloshed some of the mixture over his mother's back.

"Mother, do you think Manlegs is preparing for esod?" Snok Snok asked, retracting the limb into the smooth wall of his flank. Manlegs was what they called Aylmer; esod was a convenient way of squeaking about entropic solar orbital disestablishmentism.

"It's hard to tell, the language barrier being what it is," Quequo said, blinking through mud. "We have tried to talk about it, but without much success. I must try again; we must both try. It would be a serious matter for him if he were not prepared – he could be suddenly converted into the carrion stage. But they must have the same sort of thing happening on the Manlegs planet."

"It won't be long now, Mother, will it?"

When she did not bother to answer, for the grorgs were trotting actively up and down her spine, Snok Snok lay and thought about that time, not far off now, when Dapdrof would leave its present sun, Saffron Smiler, for Yellow Scowler. That would be a hard period, and he would need to be male and fierce and tough. Then even-tually would come Welcome White, the happy star, the sun beneath which he had been born (and which accounted for his lazy and sunny good nature); under Welcome White, he could afford to take on the cares and joys of

10

motherhood, and rear and train a son just like himself.

Ah, but life was wonderful when you thought deeply about it. The facts of esod might seem prosaic to some, but to Snok Snok, though he was only a simple country boy (simply reared too, without any notions about joining the priesthood and sailing out into the star-realms), there was a glory about nature. Even the sun's warmth, that filled his eight-hundred-and-fifty pound bulk, held a poetry incapable of paraphrase. He heaved himself to one side and excreted into the midden, as a small tribute to his mother. Do to others as you would be dung by.

"Mother, was it because the priesthood had dared to leave the worlds of the Triple Suns that they met the Manlegs Earthmen?"

"You're in a talkative mood this morning. Why don't you go in and talk to Manlegs? You know how his version of what happens in star-realms amuses you."

"But, Mother, which version is true, his or ours?"

She hesitated before giving him her answer; it was a wretchedly difficult answer, yet only through it lay an understanding of the world of affairs. She said: "Frequently there are several versions of truth."

He brushed the remark aside.

"But it was the priesthood that went beyond the Triple Suns who first met the Manlegs, wasn't it?"

"Why don't you lie still and ripen up?"

"Didn't you tell me they met on a world called Grudgrodd, only a few years after I was born?"

"Ainson told you that in the first place."

"It was you who told me that trouble would come from the meeting."

The first encounter between utod and man occurred ten years after the birth of Snok Snok. As Snok Snok said, this encounter was staged on the planet his race called Grudgrodd. Had it happened on a different planet, had

11

different protagonists been involved, the outcome of the whole matter might have been other than it was. Had someone ... but there is little point in embarking on conditionals. There are no "ifs" in history, only in the minds of observers reviewing it, and for all the progress we make, nobody has proved that chance is other than a statistical delusion invented by man. We can only say that events between man and utod fell out in such and such a way.

This narrative will chronicle these events with as little comment as possible, leaving the reader on his honour to remember that what Quequo said applies as much to man as to aliens: truths arrive in as many forms as lies.

Grudgrodd looked tolerable enough to the first utods who inspected it.

A utodian star-realm-ark had landed in a wide valley, inhospitable, rocky, cold, and covered with knee-high thistles for the greater part of its length, but nevertheless closely resembling some of the benighted spots one happened on in the northern hemisphere of Dapdrof. A pair of grorgs were sent out through the hatch, to return in half an hour intact and breathing heavily. Odds were, the place was habitable.

Ceremonial filth was shovelled out on to the ground and the Sacred Cosmopolitan was induced to excrete out of the hatch, in the universal gesture of fertility.

"I think it's a mistake," he said. The utodian for "a mistake" was Grudgrodd (as far as an atonal grunt can be rendered at all into terrestrial script), and from then on the planet was known as Grudgrodd.

Still inclined to protest, the Cosmopolitan stepped out, followed by his three Politans, and the planet was claimed as an appendage of the Triple Suns.

Four priestlings scurried busily about, clearing a circle in the thistles on the edge of the river. With all their six limbs deretracted, they worked swiftly, two of them scooping soil out of the circle, and then allowing the water to trickle in from one side, while the other two trod the resulting mud into a rich rebarbative treacle.

Watching the work abstractedly with his rear eyes, the Cosmopolitan stood on the edge of the growing crater and argued as strongly as ever a utod could on the rights and wrongs of landing on a planet not of the Triple Suns. As strongly as they could, the three Politans argued back.

"The Sacred Feeling is quite clear," said the Cosmopolitan. "As children of the Triple Suns, our defecations must touch no planets unlit by the Triple Suns; there are limits to all things, even fertility." He extended a limb upwards, where a large mauve globe as big as an ammp fruit peered coldly at them over a bank of cloud. "Is that apology for a sun Saffron Smiler? Do you take it for Welcome White? Can you even mistake it for Yellow Scowler? No, no, my friends, that mauve misery is an alien, and we waste our substance on it."

The first Politan said, "Every word you say is incontrovertible. But we are not here entirely by option. We ran into a star-realm turbulence that carried us several thousand orbits off course. This planet just happened to be our nearest haven."

"As usual you speak only the truth," the Cosmopolitan said. "But we needn't have landed here. A month's flight would have taken us back to the Triple Suns and Dapdrof, or one of her sister planets. It does seem a bit unholy of us."

"I don't think you need worry too much about that, Cosmopolitan," said the second Politan. He had the heavy greyish green skin of one born while an esod was actually taking place, and was perhaps the easiest going of all the priesthood. "Look at it this way. The Triple Suns round which Dapdrof revolve only form three of the six stars in the Home Cluster. Those six stars possess between them eight worlds capable of supporting life as we know it. After Dapdrof, we count the other seven worlds as equally

13

holy and fit for utodammp, though some of them – Buskey for instance – revolve round one of the three lesser stars of the cluster. So the criterion of what is utodammp-worthy is not that it has to revolve about one of the Triple Suns. Now we ask —"

But the Cosmopolitan, who was a better speaker than a listener, as befitted a utod in his position, cut his companion short.

"Let us ask no more, friend. I just observed that it seemed a bit unholy of us. I didn't mean any criticism. But we are setting a precedent." He scratched his grorg judicially.

With great tolerance, the third Politan (whose name was Blue Lugug) said, "I agree with every word you say, Cosmopolitan. But we do not know if we are setting a precedent. Our history is so long that it may be that many and many a crew branched out into the star-realm and there, on some far planet, set up a new swamp to the glory of utodammp. Why, if we look around, we may even find utods established here."

"You persuade me utterly; in the Revolution Age, such a thing could easily have happened," said the Cosmopolitan, in relief. Stretching out all six of his limbs, he waved them ceremonially to include ground and sky. "I pronounce all this to be land belonging to the Triple Suns. Let defecation commence."

They were happy. They grew even happier. And who could not be happy? With ease and fertility at hand, they were at home.

The mauve sun disappeared in disgrace, and almost at once a snowball-bright satellite wearing a rakish halo of dust sprang out of the horizon and rose swiftly above them. Used to great changes of temperature, the eight utods did not mind the increasing cold of night. In their newly-built wallow, they wallowed. Their sixteen attendant grorgs wallowed with them, clinging with sucker fingers

14

tenaciously to their hosts when the utods submerged beneath the mud.

Slowly they imbibed the feel of the new world. It lapped at their bodies, yielded up meanings incapable of translation into their terms.

In the sky overhead gleamed the Home Cluster, six stars arranged in the shape – or so the least intellectual of the priestling claimed – of one of the grails that swam the tempestuous seas of Smeksmer.

"We needn't have worried," said the Cosmopolitan happily. "The Triple Suns are still shining on us here. We needn't hurry back at all. Perhaps at the end of the week we'll plant a few ammp seeds and then move homewards."

". . . Or at the end of the week after next," said the third Politan, comfortable in his mud bath.

To complete their contentment, the Cosmopolitan gave them a brief religious address. They lay and listened to the web of his discourse as it was spun out of his eight orifices. He pointed out how the ammp trees and the utods were dependent upon each other, how the yield of the one depended on the yield of the other. He dwelt on the significances of the word "yield" before going on to point out how both the trees and the utods (both being the manifestations of one spirit) depended on the light yield that poured from whichever of the Triple Suns they moved about. This light was the droppings of the suns, which made it a little absurd as well as miraculous. They should never forget, any of them, that they also partook of the absurd as well as the miraculous. They must never get exalted or puffed up; for were not even their gods formed in the divine shape of a turdling?

The third Politan much enjoyed this monologue. What is most familiar is most reassuring.

He lay with only the tip of one snout showing above the bubbling surface of the mud, and spoke in his submerged voice, through his ockpu orifices. With one of his unsubmerged eyes, he gazed across at the dark bulk of their star-realm-ark, beautifully bulbous and black against the sky. Ah, life was good and rich, even so far away from beloved Dapdrof. Come next esod, he'd really have to change sex and become a mother; he owed it to his line; but even that ... well, as he'd often heard his mother say, to a pleasant mind all was pleasant. He thought lovingly of his mother, and leant against her. He was as fond of her as ever since she had changed sex and become a Sacred Cosmopolitan.

Then he squealed through all orifices.

Behind the ark, lights were flashing.

The third Politan pointed this out to his companions. They all looked where he indicated.

Not lights only. A continuous growling noise.

Not only one light. Four round sources of light, cutting through the dark, and a fifth light that moved about restlessly, like a fumbling limb. It came to rest on the ark.

"I suggest that a life form is approaching," said one of the priestlings.

As he spoke, they saw more clearly. Heading along the valley towards them were two chunky shapes. From the chunky shapes came the growling noise. The chunky shapes reached the ark and stopped. The growling noise stopped.

"How interesting! They are larger than we are," said the first Politan.

Smaller shapes were climbing from the two chunky objects. Now the light that had bathed the ark turned its eye on to the wallow. In unison, to avoid being dazzled, the utods moved their vision to a more comfortable radiation band. They saw the smaller shapes – four of them there were, and thin-shaped – line up on the bank.

"If they make their own light, they must be fairly intelligent," said the Cosmopolitan. "Which do you think the

16

life forms are – the two chunky objects with eyes, or the four thin things?"

"Perhaps the thin things are their grorgs," suggested a priestling.

"It would be only polite to get out and see," said the Cosmopolitan. He heaved his bulk up and began to move towards the four figures. His companions rose to follow him. They heard noises coming from the figures on the bank, which were now backing away.

"How delightful!" exclaimed the second Politan, hurrying to get ahead. "I do believe they are trying in their primitive way to communicate!"

"What fortune that we came!" said the third Politan, but the remark was, of course, not aimed at the Cosmopolitan.

"Greetings, creatures!" bellowed two of the priestlings.

And it was at that moment that the creatures on the bank raised Earth-made weapons to their hips and opened fire.

CHAPTER TWO

CAPTAIN BARGERONE struck a characteristic posture. Which is to say that he stood very still with his hands hanging limply down the seams of his sky blue shorts and rendered his face without expression. It was a form of self-control he had practised several times on this trip, particularly when confronted by his Master Explorer.

"Do you wish me to take what you are saying seriously,

Ainson?" he asked. "Or are you merely trying to delay take-off?"

Master Explorer Bruce Ainson swallowed; he was a religious man, and he silently summoned the Almighty to help him get the better of this fool who saw nothing beyond his duty.

"The two creatures we captured last night have definitely attempted to communicate with me, sir. Under space exploration definitions, anything that attempts to communicate with a man must be regarded as at least sub-human until proved otherwise."

"That is so, Captain Bargerone," Explorer Phipps said, fluttering his eyelashes nervously as he rose to the support of his boss.

"You do not need to assure me of the truth of platitudes, Mr. Phipps," the Captain said. "I merely question what you mean by 'attempt to communicate'. No doubt when you threw the creatures cabbage the act might have been interpreted as an attempt to communicate."

"The creatures did not throw me a cabbage, sir," Ainson said. "They stood quietly on the other side of the bars and spoke to me."

The captain's left eyebrow arched like a foil being tested by a master fencer.

"Spoke, Mr. Ainson? In an Earth language? In Portuguese, or perhaps Swahili?"

"In their own language, Captain Bargerone. A series of whistles, grunts, and squeaks often rising above audible level. Nevertheless, a language – possibly a language vastly more complex than ours."

"On what do you base that deduction, Mr. Ainson?"

The Master Explorer was not floored by the question, but the lines gathered more thickly about his rough-hewn and sorrowful face.

"On observation. Our men surprised eight of those creatures, sir, and promptly shot six of them. You should have read the patrol report. The other two creatures were so stunned by surprise that they were easily netted and brought back here into the *Mariestopes*. In the circumstances, the preoccupation of any form of life would be to seek mercy, or release if possible. In other words, it would supplicate. Unfortunately, up till now we have met no other form of intelligent life in the pocket of the galaxy near Earth; but all human races supplicate in the same way – by using gesture as well as verbal plea. These creatures do not use gesture; their language must be so rich in nuance that they have no need for gesture, even when begging for their lives."

Captain Bargerone gave an excruciatingly civilized snort.

"Then you can be sure that they were not begging for their lives. Just what did they do, apart from whining as caged dogs would do?"

"I think you should come down and see them for yourself, sir. It might help you to see things differently."

"I saw the dirty creatures last night and have no need to see them again. Of course I recognize that they form a valuable discovery; I said as much to the patrol leader. They will be off-loaded at the London Exozoo, Mr. Ainson, as soon as we get back to Earth, and then you can talk to them as much as you wish. But as I said in the first place, and as you know, it is time for us to leave this planet straight away; I can allow you no further time for exploration. Kindly remember this is a private Company ship, not a Corps ship, and we have a timetable to keep to. We've wasted a whole week on this miserable globe without finding a living thing larger than a mouse-dropping, and I cannot allow you another twelve hours here."

Bruce Ainson drew himself up. Behind him, Phipps sketched an unnoticed pastiche of the gesture.

"Then you must leave without me, sir. And without Phipps. Unfortunately, neither of us was on the patrol last night, and it is essential that we investigate the spot where these creatures were captured. You must see that the whole point of the expedition will be lost if we have no idea of their habitat. Knowledge is more important than time-tables."

"There is a war on, Mr. Ainson, and I have my orders."

"Then you will have to leave without me, sir. I don't know how the USGN will like that."

The Captain knew how to give in without appearing beaten.

"We leave in six hours, Mr. Ainson. What you and your subordinate do until then is your affair."

"Thank you, sir," said Ainson. He gave it as much edge as he dared.

Hurrying from the captain's office, he and Phipps caught a lift down to disembarkation deck and walked down the ramp on to the surface of the planet provisionally label-led 12B.

The men's canteen was still functioning. With sure instinct, the two explorers marched in to find the members of the Exploration Corps who had been involved in the events of the night before. The canteen was of pre-formed reinplast and served the synthetic foods so popular on Earth. At one table sat a stocky young American with a fresh face, a red neck, and a razor-sharp crewcut. His name was Hank Quilter, and the more perceptive of his friends had him marked down as a man who would go far. He sat over a synthwine (made from nothing so vulgar as a grape grown from the coarse soil and ripened by the un-refined elements) and argued, his surly-cheerful face animated as he scorned the viewpoint of Ginger Duffield, the ship's weedy messdeck lawyer.

Ainson broke up the conversation without ceremony. Quilter had led the patrol of the previous night.

Draining his glass, Quilter resignedly fetched a thin youth named Walthamstone who had also been on the patrol, and the four of them walked over to the motor pool – being demolished amid shouting perparatory to take-off – to collect an overlander.

Ainson signed for the vehicle, and they drove off with Walthamstone at the wheel and Phipps distributing weapons. The latter said, "Bargerone hasn't given us much time, Bruce. What do you hope to find?"

"I want to examine the site where the creatures were captured. Of course I would like to find something that would make Bargerone eat humble pie." He caught Phipps' warning glance at the men and said sharply, "Quilter, you were in charge last night. Your trigger-finger was a bit itchy, wasn't it? Did you think you were in the Wild West?"

Quilter turned round to give his superior a look.

"Captain complimented me this morning," was all he said.

Dropping that line of approach, Ainson said, "These beasts may not look intelligent, but if one is sensitive one can *feel* a certain something about them. They show no panic, nor fear of any kind."

"Could be as much a sign of stupidity as intelligence," Phipps said.

"Mm, possible, I suppose. All the same. ... Another thing, Gussie, that seems worth pursuing. Whatever the standing of these creatures may be, they don't fit with the larger animals we've discovered on other planets so far. Oh, I know we've only found a couple of dozen planets harbouring any sort of life – dash it, star travel isn't thirty years old yet. But it does seem as if light gravity planets breed light spindly beings and heavy planets breed bulky compact beings. And these critters are exceptions to the rule."

"I see what you mean. This world has not much more mass than Mars, yet our bag are built like rhinoceroses."

"They were all wallowing in the mud like rhinos when

21

we found them," Quilter offered. "How could they have any intelligence?"

"You shouldn't have shot them down like that. They must be rare, or we'd have spotted some elsewhere on 12B before this."

"You don't stop to think when you're on the receiving end of a rhino charge," Quilter sulked.

"So I see."

They rumbled over an unkempt plain in silence. Ainson tried to recapture the happiness he had experienced on first walking across this untrod planet. New planets always renewed his pleasure in life; but such pleasures had been spoiled this voyage – spoiled as usual by other people. He had been mistaken to ship on a Company boat; life on Space Corps boats was more rigid and simple; unfortunately, the Anglo-Brazilian war engaged all Corps ships, keeping them too busy with solar system manœuvres for such peaceful enterprises as exploration. Nevertheless, he did not deserve a captain like Edgar Bargerone.

Pity Bargerone did not blast-off and leave him here by himself, Ainson thought. Away from people, communing – he recollected his father's phrase – communing with nature!

The people would come to 12B. Soon enough it would have, like Earth, its over-population problems. That was why it was explored: with a view to colonization. Sites for the first communities had been marked out on the other side of the world. In a couple of years, the poor wretches forced by economic necessity to leave all they held dear on Earth would be trans-shipped to 12B (but they would have a pretty and tempting colonial name for it by then: Clementine, or something equally obnoxiously innocuous).

Yes, they'd tackle this unkempt plain with all the pluck of their species, turning it into a heaven of dirt-farming and semi-detacheds. Fertility was the curse of the human race, Ainson thought. Too much procreation went on;

Earth's teeming loins had to ejaculate once again, ejaculate its unwanted progeny on to the virgin planets that lay awaiting – well, awaiting what else?

Christ, what else? There must be something else, or we should all have stayed in the nice green harmless Pleistocene.

Ainson's rancid thoughts were broken by Walthamstone's saying, "There's the river. Just round the corner, and then we're there."

They rounded low banks of gravel from which thorn trees grew. Overhead, a mauve sun gleamed damply through haze at them. It raised a shimmer of reflection from the leaves of a million million thistles, growing silently all the way to the river and on the other side of it as far as the eye wanted to see. Only one landmark: a big blunt odd-shaped thing straight ahead.

"It – " said Phipps and Ainson together. They stared at each other. " – looks like one of the creatures."

"The mudhole where we caught them is just the other side," Walthamstone said. He bumped the overlander across the thistle bed, braking in the shadow of the looming object, forlorn and strange as a chunk of Liberian carving lying on an Aberdeen mantelshelf.

Toting their rifles, they jumped out and moved forward.

They stood on the edge of the mudhole and surveyed it. One side of the circle was sucked by the grey lips of the river. The mud itself was brown and pasty green, streaked liberally with red where five big carcasses took their last wallow in the carefree postures of death. The sixth body gave a heave and turned a head in their direction.

A cloud of flies rose in anger at this disturbance. Quilter brought up his rifle, turning a grim face to Ainson when the latter caught his arm.

"Don't kill it," Ainson said. "It's wounded. It can't harm us."

"We can't assume that. Let me finish it off."

23

"I said not, Quilter. We'll get it into the back of the overlander and take it to the ship; we'd better collect the dead ones too. Then they can be cut up and their anatomy studied. They'd never forgive us on Earth if we lost such an opportunity. You and Walthamstone get the nets out of the lockers and haul the bodies up."

Quilter looked challengingly at his watch and at Ainson.

"Get moving," Ainson ordered.

Reluctantly, Walthamstone slouched forward to do as he was told; unlike Quilter, he was not of the stuff from which rebels are made. Quilter curled his lip and followed. They hauled the nets out and went to stand on the edge of the mud pool, gazing across it at the half-submerged evidence of last night's activities before they got down to work. The sight of the carnage mollified Quilter.

"We sure stopped them!" he said. He was a muscular young man, with his fair hair neatly cropped and a dear old white-haired mother back home in Miami who pulled in an annual fortune in alimony.

"Yeah. They'd have got us otherwise," Walthamstone said. "Two of them I shot myself. Must have been those two nearest to us."

"I killed two of them, too," Quilter said. "They were all wallowing in the mud like rhinos. Boy, did they come at us!"

"Dirty things when you come to look at them. Ugly. Worse than anything we've got on Earth. Aren't half glad we plugged them, aren't you, Quil?"

"It was us or them. We didn't have any choice."

"You're right there." Walthamstone cuddled his chin and looked admiringly at his friend. You had to admit Quilter was quite a lad. He repeated Quilter's phrase, "We didn't have any choice."

"What the hell good are they, I'd like to know."

"So'd I. We really stopped them, though, didn't we?"

"It was us or them," repeated Quilter. The flies rose

again as he paddled into the mud towards the wounded rhinoman.

While this philosophical skirmish was in progress, Bruce Ainson stalked over to the object that marked the scene of the slaughter. It loomed above him. He was impressed. This shape, like the shape of the creatures it appeared to imitate, had more than its size to impress him; there was something about it that affected him aesthetically It might be a hundred light years high and it'd still be – don't say beauty doesn't exist! – beautiful.

He climbed into the beautiful object. It stank to high heaven; and that was where it had been intended for. Five minutes' inspection left him in no doubt: this was a ... well, it looked like an overgrown seedpod, and it had the feel of an overgrown seedpod, but it was – Captain Bargerone had to see this: this was a space ship.

A space ship loaded high with shit.

CHAPTER THREE

MUCH happened during the year 1999 on Earth. Quins were born to a twenty-year-old mother in Kennedyville, Mars. A robot team was admitted for the first time into the World series. New Zealand launched its own system-ship. The first Spanish nuclear submarine was launched by a Spanish princess. There were two one-day revolutions in Java, six in Sumatra, and seven in South America. Brazil declared war on Great Britain. Common Europe beat the U.S.S.R. at football. A Japanese screen star married the Shah of Persia. The gallant All-Texan expedition attempting to cross the bright side of Mercury in exotanks perished to a man. All-Africa set up its first radio-controlled whale farm. And a little grizzled Australian mathematician called Buzzard rushed into his mistress's room at three o'clock of a May morning shrieking, "Got it, got it! Transponential flight!"

Within two years, the first unmanned and experimental transponential drive had been built into a rocket, launched, and proved successful. They never got that one back.

This is not the place for an explanation of TP formulae; the printer, in any case, refuses to set three pages of math symbols. Suffice it to say that a favourite science fiction gimmick – to the dismay and subsequent bankruptcy of all science fiction writers – was suddenly translated into actuality. Thanks to Buzzard, the gulfs of space became not barriers between but doorways to the planets. By 2010, you could get from New York to Procyon more comfortably and quickly than it had taken, a century before, to get from New York to Paris.

That is what's so tedious about progress. Nobody seems able to jog it out of that dreary old exponential curve.

All of which goes to show that while the trip between B12 and Earth took less than a fortnight by the year 2035, that still left plenty of time for letter writing.

Or – in Captain Bargerone's case, as he composed a TP cable to their lordships in the Admiralty – for cable writing.

In the first week he cabled:

TP POSITION: 355073x 6915 (B12). YOUR CABLE EX 97747304 REFERS. YOUR ORDER COMPLIED WITH. HENCEFORTH CREATURES CAPTIVE ABOARD KNOWN AS EXTRATERRESTIAL ALIENS (SHORTENED TO ETAS).

SITUATION REGARDING ETAS AS FOLLOWS: TWO ALIVE

AND WELL IN NUMBER THREE HOLD. OTHER CARCASSES BEING DISSECTED TO STUDY THEIR ANATOMY. AT FIRST I DID NOT REALIZE THEY WERE MORE THAN ANIMALS. DIRECTLY MASTER EXPLORER AINSON EXPLAINED SITUATION TO ME, I ORDERED HIM TO PROCEED WITH PARTY TO SCENE OF CAPTURE OF ETAS.

THERE WE FOUND EVIDENCE THAT ETAS HAVE INTELLIGENCE. SPACE SHIP OF STRANGE MANUFACTURE WAS TAKEN INTO CUSTODY. IT IS NOW IN MAIN CARGO HOLD AFTER REDISTRIBUTION OF CARGO. SMALL SHIP CAPABLE OF HOLDING ONLY FIGURE 8 ETAS. NO DOUBT SHIP BELONGS ETAS. SAME FILTH OVER EVERYTHING. SAME OFFENSIVE SMELL. EVIDENCE SUGGESTS THAT ETAS ALSO EXPLORING B12.

HAVE ORDERED AINSON AND HIS STAFF TO COMMUNICATE WITH ETAS SOONEST. HOPE TO HAVE LANGUAGE PROBLEM CRACKED BEFORE LANDING.

> EDGAR BARGERONE. CAPT. MARIESTOPES.
> GMT 1750:6.7.2035.

Other prosodists were busy aboard the *Mariestopes*.

Walthamstone wrote laboriously to an aunt in a far-flung western suburb of London called Windsor:

My dear old aunt Flo –

We are now coming home to see you again, how is your ruhmatism, looking up I hope. I have not been space sick this voyage. When the ship goes into TP drive if you know what this is you feel a bit sick for a couple of hours. My pal Quilt says that's because all your molecules go negative. But then you're all right.

When we stopped at one planet which hasn't got no name because we were the first, Quilt and me had a chance to go hunting. The place is swarming with big fierce dirty animals as big as the ship. It lives in mudholes. We shot dozens. We got two alive ones on board this old tub, we call them rhinomen, their names are Gertie and Mush. They are filthy. I have to clean out their cage but they don't bite. They make a lot of rude noises.

As usual the food is bad. Not only poison but small helpings. Give my love to cousin Madge, I wonder if her edducation is completed yet. Whose winning the war with Brazil, us I hope!!!!

Hoping this leaves you as it finds me at present, your loving nephew,

RODNEY.

Augustus Phipps was composing a love letter to a Sino-Portuguese girl; above his bunk was a phobe of her looking extremely sinuous. Phipps regarded it frequently as he wrote:

Ah Chi darling,

This brave old bus is now pointing towards Macao. My heart as you know is permanently oriented (no pun intended) towards that fair place when you are holidaying there, but how good to know we shall soon be together in more than spirit.

I'm hoping this trip will bring us fame and fortune. For we have found a sort of strange life out here in this neck of the galaxy, and are bringing two live samples of it home. When I think of you, so slender, sweet, and immaculate in your cheongsam, I wonder why we need such dirty ugly beasts on the same planet – but science must be served.

Wonder of wonders! – They're supposed to be intelligent according to my superior, and we are presently engaged in trying to talk to them. No, don't laugh, pretty though I remember your laughter to be. How I long for the moment I can talk to you, my sweet and passionate Ah Chi; and of course not only talk! You must let me [Ed. – two pages omitted].

Until we can do the same sort of thing again,

Your devoted
adoring
admiring
pulsating
AUGUSTUS.

Meanwhile, down on the messdeck of the *Mariestopes*, Quilter also was wrestling with the problem of communicating with a girl:

Hi honey!

Right now as I write I am heading straight back to Dodge City as fast as the light waves will carry me. Got the captain and the boys along with me too, but I'll be shedding them before I drop in at 1477 Rainbow.

Beneath a brave exterior, your lover boy is feeling sour way up to here. These beasts, the rhinomen I was telling you about, they are the filthiest things you ever saw, and I can't tell you about it in the mails. Guess it's because you like me I know have always taken a pride in being modern and hygienic, but these things they're worse than animals.

This has finished me for the Exploration Corps. At trip's end, I quit and shall remuster in the Space Corps. You can go places in the Space Corps. As witness our Captain Bargerone, jumped up from nowhere. His father is caretaker or something at a block of flats Amsterdam way. Well, that's democracy – guess I'll try some myself, maybe wind up captain myself. Why not?

This seems to be written all around me, honey. When I get home you bet I'll be all around you.

Your lovingest chewingest

HANK.

In his cabin on B deck, Master Explorer Bruce Ainson wrote soberly to his wife:

My dearest Enid,

How often I pray that your ordeal with Aylmer may now be over. You have done all you could for the boy, never reproach yourself on that score. He is a disgrace to our name. Heaven alone knows what will become of him. I fear he is as dirty-minded as he is dirty in his personal habits.

My regret is that I have to be away so long, particularly

when a son of ours is causing so much trouble. But a consolation is that at last this trip has become rewarding. We have located a major life form. Under my supervision, two live individuals of this form have been brought aboard this ship. ETA's we call them.

You will be considerably more surprised when I tell you that these individuals, despite their strange appearance and habits, appear to manifest intelligence. More than that, they seem to be a space-faring race. We captured a space ship that undoubtedly is connected with them, though whether they actually control the craft is at present undecided. I am attempting to communicate with them, but as yet without success.

Let me describe the ETA's to you – rhinomen, the crew call them, and until a better designation is arrived at, that will do. The rhinomen walk on six limbs. The six limbs each terminate in very capable hands, widespread, but each bearing six digits, of which the first and last are opposed and may be regarded as thumbs. The rhinomen are omnidextrous. When not in use, the limbs are retracted into the hide rather like a tortoise's legs, and are then barely noticeable.

With its limbs retracted, a rhinoman is symmetrical and shaped roughly like the two segments of an orange adhering together, the shallow curve representing the creature's spine, the fuller curve its belly, and the two apices its two heads. Yes, our captives appear to be two-headed; the heads come to a point and are neckless, though they can swivel through several degrees. In each head are set two eyes, small and dark in colour with lower lids that slide upward to cover the eyes during sleep. Beneath the eyes are orifices which look alike; one is the rhinoman's mouth, one his anus. There are also several orifices punctuating the expanse of body; these may be breathing tubes. The exobiologists are dissecting some corpses we have aboard with us. When I get their report, several things should be clearer.

Our captives encompass a wide range of sounds, ranging through whistles and screams to grunts and smacking noises. I fear that all orifices are able to contribute to this gamut of sound, some of which, I am convinced, goes above man's auditory threshold. As yet neither of our specimens is communicative, though all the sounds they make to each other are automatically recorded on tape; but I am sure this is merely due to the shock of capture, and that on Earth, with more time, and in a more congenial environment where we can keep them more hygienically, we shall soon begin to obtain positive results.

As ever, these long voyages are tedious. I avoid the captain as much as I can; an unpleasant man, with public school and Cambridge written all over him. I immerse myself in our two ETA's. For all their unpleasant habits, they have a fascination my human companions lack.

There will be much to talk about on my return.

Your dutiful husband,

BRUCE.

Down in the main cargo hold, safely away from all the letter-writing, a mixed bag of men of all trades was stripping the ETA space ship and pulling it to pieces splinter by splinter. For the strange craft was made of wood, wood of an unknown toughness, wood of an unknown resilience, wood as tough and durable as steel – yet wood which on the inside, for it was shaped like a great pod, sprouted a variety of branches like horns. On these branches grew a lowly type of parasitic plant. One of the triumphs of the botanical team was the discovery that this parasite was not the natural foliage of the horn-branches but an alien growing thereon.

They also discover that the parasite was a glutton for absorbing carbon dioxide from the air and exuding oxygen. They scraped bits of the parasite from the horn-branches and attempted to grow it in more favourable conditions; the plant died. At the current one hundred and thirty-fourth attempt, it was still dying, but the men in Bot were noted for stubbornness.

The interior of the ship was caked with filth of a certain rich consistency made up chiefly of mud and excrement. When comparing this dirty little wooden coracle with the gleamingly clean *Mariestopes*, it would have been impossible for an rational individual – and rational individuals exist even amid the incarcerations of space travel – to imagine that both craft were constructed for the same purpose. Indeed, many of the crew, and notably those who prided themselves on their rationality, were loud in their laughter as they refused to concede that the alien artifact was anything but a well-frequented jakes.

Discovering the drive quenched about 98 per cent of the laughter. Under the mire the motor lay, a strange distorted thing no bigger than a rhinoman. It was snugged into the wooden hull without visible welding and bolting; it was made of a substance outwardly resembling porcelain; it had no moving parts; and a ceramicist followed it weeping with a wild surmise into the engineering labs when the unit was finally drilled and grilled from the hull.

The next discovery was a bunch of great nuts that clung to the two peaks of the roof with a tenacity that defied the best flame-cutters. At least, some said they were nuts, for a fibrous husk covering them suggested the fruits of the coconut palm. But when it was perceived that the ribs running down from the nuts which had hitherto been regarded as wall strengtheners connected with the drive, several sages declared the nuts to be fuel tanks.

The next discovery put an end to discoveries for a time. An artisan chipping at a hardened bank of dirt discovered, entombed within it, a dead ETA. Thereupon the men gathered together and made emotional noises.

"How much longer are we going to stand for this, fellows?" cried Interior Rating Ginger Duffield, jumping on to a tool box and showing them white teeth and black fists. "This is a company ship, not a Corps ship, and we don't have to put up with just any old treatment they care to give us. There's nothing down in regulations says we have to clean out alien tombs and bogs. I'm downing tools till we get Dirty Pay, and I demand you lot join me."

His words drew forth a babble of response.

"Yes, make the company pay!"

"Who do they think they are?"

"Let 'em clean out their own stink holes!"

"More pay! Time and a half, boys!"

"Get knotted, Duffield, you ruddy trouble-maker."

"What does the sergeant say?"

Sergeant Warrick elbowed his way through the bunch of men. He stood looking up at Ginger Duffield, whose lean and peppery figure did not wilt under the gaze.

"Duffield, I know your sort. You ought to be out on the Deep Freeze Planet, helping to win the war. We don't want none of your factory tactics here. Climb down off that box and let's all get back to work. A bit of dirt won't harm your lily white hands."

Duffield spoke very quietly and nicely.

"I'm not looking for any trouble, sarge. Why should we do it, that's all I say. Don't know what dangerous disease is lurking in this little cesspit. We want danger money for working in it. Why should we risk our necks for the company? What's the company ever done for us?" A rumble of approval greeted this question, but Duffield affected to take no notice of it. "What're they going to do when we get home? Why, they're going to put this stinking alien box on show, and everyone's going to come and have a look and a sniff at ten tubbies a time. They're going to make their fortune out of this and out of those animals that lived in it. So why shouldn't we have our little bite now? You just push along to C Deck and bring the Union

33

man to see us, hey, sarge, and keep that nose of yours out of trouble, hey?"

"You're nothing but a flaming trouble-maker, Duffield, that's your trouble," the sergeant said angrily. He pushed through the men, heading for C Deck. Mocking cheers followed him into the corridor.

Two watches later, Quilter, armed with hose and brush, entered the cage containing the two ETA's. They sprouted their limbs and moved to the far end of the confined space, watching him hopefully.

"This is the last clean-out you guys are going to get from me," Quilter told them. "At the end of this watch, I'm joining the walk-out, just to demonstrate my solidarity with the Space Corps. After this, as far as I'm concerned, you can sleep in crap as deep as the Pacific."

With the fun-loving ebullience of youth, he turned the hose on to them.

CHAPTER FOUR

THE news editor of the *Windsor Circuit* struck the pedal bar of his technivision and scowled at the representation of his chief reporter's face as it appeared on the screen.

"Where the hell are you, Adrian? Get down to the bloody spaceport as you were told. The *Mariestopes* is due within half an hour."

The left half of Adrian Bucker's countenance screwed

itself into a wince. He leant nearer to his screen until his nose opaqued and the vision misted and said, "Don't be like that, Ralph. I've got a local angle on the trip that you'll fairly lap up."

"I don't want a local angle, I want you down at that ruddy spaceport right away, my lad."

Bucker winced the right side of his face and began talking fast.

"Listen, Ralph. I'm in 'The Angel's Head' – the pub right on the Thames. I've got an old girl here called Florence Walthamstone. She's lived in Windsor all her life, remembers when the Great Park was a park, all that sort of stuff. She's got a nephew called Rodney Walthamstone who's a rating on the *Mariestopes*. She's just been showing me a letter from him in which he describes these alien animals they're bringing home, and I thought that if we ran a picture of her, with a quote from the letter – you know, Local Lad Helps Capture Those Monsters – it would look —"

"That's enough, I've heard enough. This thing's the biggest news of the decade and you imagine we need a local angle to put it over? Give the old girl her letter back, thank her very much for the offer, pay for her drink, pat her dear wrinkled cheeks, and then get down to that bloody spaceport and interview Bargerone or I'll have your skin for flypaper."

"Okay, okay, Ralph, have it the way you want it. There was a time when you were open to suggestions." Having cut the circuit, Bucker added, "And I've got one I could make right now."

He pushed out of the booth, and jostled his way through a heavy-bodied, heavy-drinking mass of men and women to a tall old woman crushed into the corner of the bar. She was lifting a glass of dark brown to her lips, her little finger genteelly cocked at an angle.

"Was your editor excited?" she asked, splashing slightly.

35

"Stood on his head. Look, Miss Walthamstone, I'm sorry about this, but I've got to get down to the spaceport. Perhaps we can do a special interview with you later. Now I've got your number; don't bother to ring us, we'll ring you, right, eh? Very nice to meet you."

As he gulped the last of his drink down, she said, "Oh, but you ought to let me pay for that one, Mr. —"

"Very kind of you, if you insist, very kind, Miss Walthamstone. 'Bye then."

He flung himself among the filling stomachs. She called his name. He looked back furiously from the middle of the fray.

"Have a word with Rodney if you see him. He'd be ever so glad to tell you anything. He's a very nice boy."

He fought his way to the door, muttering, "Excuse me, excuse me," over and over, like a curse.

The reception bays at the spaceport were crowded. Ordinary and extraordinary citizens packed every roof and window. In a roped-off section of the tarmac stood representatives of various governments, including the Minister for Martian Affairs, and of various services, including the Director of the London Exozoo. Beyond the enclosure, the band of a well-known regiment, uniformed in anachronistically bright colours, marched about playing Suppé's Light Cavalry Overture and selections of Irish melodies. Ice cream was hawked, newspapers were sold, pockets were picked. The *Mariestopes* slid through a layer of nimbostratus and settled on its haunches in a distant part of the field.

It began to rain.

The band embarked on a lively rendering of the twentieth-century air "Sentimental Journey" without adding much lustre to the proceedings. As such occasions usually are, this occasion was dull, its interest diffused. The spraying of the entire hull of the ship with germicidal sprays took some while. A hatch opened, a little overalled figure appeared in the opening, was cheered, and disappeared again. A thousand children asked if that was Captain Bargerone and were told not to be silly.

At length a ramp came out like a reluctant tongue and lolled against the ground. Transport – three small buses, two trucks, an ambulance, various luggage tenders, a private car, and several military vehicles – converged on to the great ship from different parts of the port. And finally a line of human beings began to move hastily down the ramp with bowed heads and dived into the shelter of the vehicles. The crowd cheered; it had come to cheer.

In a reception hall, the gentlemen of the press had made the air blue with the smoke of their mescahales before Captain Bargerone was thrust in upon them. Flashes sizzled and danced as he smiled defensively at them.

With some of his officers standing behind him, he stood and spoke quietly and unsensationally in a very English way (Bargerone was French) about how much space there was out there and how many worlds there were and how devoted his crew had been except for an unfortunate strike on the way home for which someone, he hoped, was going to get it hot; and he finished by saying that on a very pleasant planet which the USGN had graciously decided should be known as Clementina they had captured or killed some large animals with interesting characteristics. Some of these characteristics he described. The animals had two heads, each of which held a brain. The two brains together weighed 2,000 grammes – a quarter more than man's. These animals, ETA's or rhinomen, as the crew called them, had six limbs which ended in undoubted equivalents of hands. Unfortunately the strike had hindered the study of the remarkable creatures, but there seemed a fair reason to suppose that they had a language of their own and must therefore, despite their ugliness and dirty habits, be regarded as more or less – but of course nobody could be certain as yet, and it might take many months of patient research before we could be certain – as an intelligent form of life on a par with man and capable of having a civilization of their own, on a planet as yet unknown to man. Two of them were preserved in captivity and would go to the Exozoo for study.

When the speech was over, reporters closed round Bargerone.

"You're saying these rhinos don't live on Clementina?"

"We have reason to suppose not."

"What reason?"

("Smile for the *Subud Times*, please, Captain.")

"We think they were on a visit there, just as we were."

"You mean they travelled in a spaceship?"

"In a sense, yes. But they may just have been taken along on the trip as experimental animals – or dumped there, like Captain Cook's pigs dumped on Tahiti or wherever it was."

("More profile, Captain, if you please.")

"Well, did you see their spaceship?"

"Er well, we think we actually have ... er, their spaceship in our hold."

"Give, then, Captain, this is big! Why the secrecy? Have you captured their spaceship or have you not?"

("And over this way, sir.")

"We think we have. That is, it has the properties of a spaceship, but it, er – no TP drive naturally, but an interesting drive, and, well, it sounds silly but you see the hull is made of wood. A very high-density wood." Captain Bargerone wiped his face clear of expression.

"Oh now look, Captain, you're joking. ..."

In the mob of photographers, phototects, and reporters, Adrian Bucker could get nowhere near the captain. He elbowed his way across to a tall nervous man who stood behind Bargerone, scowling out of one of the long windows at the crowds milling about in the light rain.

"Would you tell me how you feel about these aliens you

brought back to Earth, sir?" Bucker asked. "Are they animals or are they people?"

Hardly hearing, Bruce Ainson sent his gaze probing over the crowds outside. He thought he had caught a glimpse of his good-for-nothing son, Aylmer, wearing his usual hangdog expression as he plunged through the mob.

"Swine," he said.

"You mean they look like swine or they act like swine?" The explorer turned to stare at the reporter.

"I'm Bucker of the *Windsor Circuit*, sir. My paper would be interested in anything you could tell us about these creatures. You think they are animals, am I right in saying?"

"What would you say mankind is, Mr. Bucker, civilized beings or animals? Have we ever met a new race without corrupting it or destroying it? Look at the Polynesians, the Guanches, the American Indians, the Tasmanians. . . ."

"Yes, sir, I get your point, but would you say these aliens. . . ."

"Oh, they have intelligence, as has any mammal; these are mammals. But their behaviour or lack of behaviour is baffling because we must not think anthropomorphically about them. Have they ethics, have they consciences? Are they capable of being corrupted as the Eskimos and Indians were? Are they perhaps capable of corrupting us? We have to ask ourselves a lot of searching questions before we are capable of seeing these rhinomen clearly. That is my feeling on the matter."

"That is very interesting. What you are saying is that we have to develop a new way of thinking, is that it?"

"No, no, no, I hardly think this is a problem I can discuss with a newspaper representative, but man places too much trust in his intellect; what we need is a new way of feeling, a more reverent. . . . I was getting somewhere with those two unhappy creatures we have captive – establishing trust, you know, after we had slaughtered their companions and taken them prisoner, and what is happening to them now? They're going to be a sideshow in the Exozoo. The Director, Sir Mihaly Pasztor, is an old friend of mine; I shall complain to him."

"Heck, people want to see the beasts! How do we know they have feelings like ours?"

"Your view, Mr. Bucker, is probably the view of the damn fool majority. Excuse me, I have a technicall to make."

Ainson hurried from the building, where the wedge of people instantly closed in and held him tight. He stood helpless there while a lorry moved slowly by, buoyed along with cheers, cries and exclamations from the onlookers. Through the bars at the back of the lorry, the two ETA's stared down on the onlookers. They made no sound. They were large and grey, beings at once forlorn and formidable.

Their gaze rested on Bruce Ainson. They gave no sign of recognition. Suddenly chilled, he turned and began to worm his way through the press of wet mackintoshes.

The ship was emptying and being emptied. Cranes dipped their great beaks into the ship's vitals, coming up with nets full of cartons, boxes, crates, and canisters. Sewage lighters swarmed, sucking out the waste from the metal creature's alimentary canal. The hull bled men in little gouts. The great whale *Mariestopes* was stranded and powerless, beached far from its starry native deeps.

Walthamstone and Ginger Duffield followed Quilter to one of the exit ducts. Quilter was loaded with kit and due to catch an ionosphere jet from another corner of the port to the U.S.A. in half an hour's time. They paused on the lip of the ship and looked out quizzically, inhaling the strange-tasting air.

"Look at it, worst weather in the universe," Walthamstone complained. "I'm staying in here till it stops, I tell you straight."

"Catch a taxi," Duffield suggested.

" 'Tisn't worth it. My aunt's place is only half a mile away. My bike's over there in the P.T.O.'s offices. I'll cycle when the rain clears – if it does."

"Does the P.T.O. let you leave your bike there free between flights?" Duffield asked with interest.

Anxious not to get involved in what promised to become a rather English conversation, Quilter shrugged a duffel bag more comfortably on to his shoulders and said, "Say, you men, come on over to the flight canteen and have a nice warm British synthbeer with me before I go."

"We ought to celebrate the fact that you have just left the Exploration Corps," Walthamstone said. "Shall we go along, Ginger?"

"Did they stamp your paybook 'Discharged' and sign you off officially?" Duffield asked.

"I only signed on on a Flight-by-flight basis," Quilter explained. "All perfectly legal, Duffield, you old barrack-room lawyer, you. Don't you ever relax?"

"You know my motto, Hank. Observe it and you won't go wrong: 'They'll twist you if they can.' I knew a bloke a bit ago who forgot to get his 535 cleared by the Quartermaster before he was demobbed, and they had him back. They did, they caught him for another five years. He's serving on Charon now, helping to win the war."

"Are you coming for this beer or aren't you?"

"I'd better come," Walthamstone said. "We may never see you again after this bird in Dodge City gets at you, from what you've told me about her. I'd run a mile from that sort of girl, myself."

He moved tentatively out into the fine drizzle; Quilter followed, glancing back over his shoulder at Duffield.

"Are you coming, Ginger, or aren't you?"

Duffield looked crafty.

"I'm not leaving this ship till I get my strike pay, mate," he said.

Explorer Phipps was home. He had embraced his

41

parents and was hanging his coat in the hall. They stood behind him, managing to look discontented even while they smiled. Shabby, round-shouldered, they gave him the grumbling welcome he knew so well. They spoke in turn, two monologues that never made a dialogue.

"Come along in the sitting-room, Gussie. It's warmer in there," his mother said. "You'll be cold after leaving the ship. I'll get a cup of tea in a minute."

"Had a bit of trouble with the central heating. Shouldn't need it now we're into June, but it has been usually chilly for the time of year. It's such a job to get anyone to come and look at anything. I don't know what's happening to people. They don't seem to want your custom nowadays."

"Tell him about the new doctor, Henry. Terribly rude man, absolutely no education or manners at all. And dirty finger-nails – fancy expecting to examine anyone with dirty finger-nails."

"Of course, it's the war that's to blame. It's brought an entirely different type of man to the surface. Brazil shows no sign of weakening, and meanwhile the government —"

"The poor boy doesn't want to hear about the war directly he gets home, Henry. They've even started rationing some foodstuffs! All we hear is propaganda, propaganda, on the techni. And the quality of things has deteriorated too. I had to buy a new saucepan last week —"

"Settle yourself down here, Gussie. Of course it's the war that's to blame. I don't know what's to become of us all. The news from Sector 160 is so depressing, isn't it?"

Phipps said, "Out in the galaxy, nobody takes any interest in the war. I must say it all sounds a bit of a shower to me."

"Haven't lost your patriotism, have you, Gussie?" his father asked.

"What's patriotism but an extension of egotism?" Phipps asked, and was glad to see his father's chest,

42

momentarily puffed, shrink again.

His mother broke a tense silence by saying, "Anyhow, dear, you'll see a difference in England while you're on leave. How long have you got, by the way?"

Little as the parental chatter enthralled Phipps, this sudden question discomforted him, as mother and father waited eagerly for his answer. He knew that stifling feeling of old. They wanted nothing of him, only that he was there to be spoken to. They wanted nothing from him but his life.

"I shall only be staying here for a week. That charming part-Chinese girl that I met last leave, Ah Chi, is in the Far East on a painting holiday. Next Thursday I fly to Macao to stay with her."

Familiarity again. He knew his father's would-be piteous shake of the head, that particular pursing of his mother's lips as if she nursed a lemon pip there. Before they could speak, he rose to his feet.

"I'll just go upstairs and unpack my grip, if you'll both excuse me."

CHAPTER FIVE

PASZTOR, Director of the London Exozoo, was a fine willowy man without a grey hair on his head despite his fifty-two years. A Hungarian by birth, he had led an expedition into the submarine Antarctic by the time he was twenty-five, had gone on to set up the Tellus Zoological Dome on the asteroid Apollo in 2005, and had written the most viewed technidrama of 2014, *An Iceberg for Icarus*. Several years later he went on the First Charon Expedition, which charted and landed upon that then newly-discovered planet of the solar system; Charon refrigerates so unloveably some three thousand million miles beyond the orbit of Pluto that it earned itself the name of Deep Freeze Planet, Pasztor had given it that nickname.

After which triumph, Sir Mihaly Pasztor was appointed Director of the London Exozoo and was at present employed in offering Bruce Ainson a drink.

"You know I don't, Mihaly," Bruce said, shaking his long head in reproof.

"From now on you are a famous man; you should toast your own success, as we toast it. The drinks are all pure synthetics, you know – a de-alcoholized sinker will surely never hurt you."

"You know me of old, Mihaly. I wish only to do my duty."

"I know you of old, Bruce. I know that you care very little for the opinions or the applause of anyone else, so thirstily do you crave for the nod of approval from your own superego," the Director said in a mild voice, while the bartender mixed him the cocktail known as a Transponential. They were at the reception being held in the hotel belonging to the Exozoo, where murals of exotic beasts stared down on a bracing mixture of bright uniforms and flowery dresses.

"I do not stand in need of titbits from your well of wisdom," Ainson said.

"You will not allow that you have need of anything from anybody," said the Director. "I have meant to say this to you for a long while, Bruce – though this is neither the time nor the place, let me continue now I have begun.

You are a brave, learned, and formidable man. That you have proved not only to the world but to yourself. You can now afford to relax, to let down your guard. Not only can you now afford to do so; you ought to do so before it is too late. A man has to have an interior, Bruce, and yours is dying of suffocation —"

"For heavens' sake, man!" Ainson exclaimed, breaking away half laughing, half angry. "You are talking like an impossibly romantic character in one of the plays of your nonage! I am what I am, and I am no different from what I have always been. Now here comes Enid, and it is high time we changed the subject."

Among the bright dresses, Enid Ainson's hooded cobra costume looked as sunny as an eclipse. She smiled, however, as she came up to her husband and Pasztor.

"This is a lovely party, Mihaly. How foolish I was not to have come to the last one, the last time Bruce came home. You have such a pretty room here to hold it in, too."

"For wartime, Enid, we try to squeeze a little extra gaiety, and your appearance has done the trick."

She laughed, obviously pleased, but compelled to protest.

"You're flattering me, Mihaly, just as you always do."

"Does your husband never flatter you?"

"Well, I don't know. ... I don't know if Bruce – I mean —"

"You're being silly, the pair of you," Ainson said. "The noise in here is enough to make anyone senseless. Mihaly, I've had enough of all this frippery, and I'm surprised that you haven't too, Enid. Let's get down to business; I came here to hand the ETA's over to you officially, and that's what I want to do. Can we discuss that in peace and quiet somewhere?"

Pasztor had trim eyebrows which rose towards his hairline, descended, and then moved together in a frown.

"Are you trying to distract me from my duty to the bartender? Well, I suppose we can slip down to the new ETA enclosure, if you must. Your specimens should be installed by now, and the spaceport officials out of the way."

Ainson turned to his wife, laying a hand on her arm.

"You come along too, Enid; the excitement up here isn't good for you."

"Nonsense, my dear, I'm enjoying myself." She removed her arm from his grasp.

"Well really, you might show a little interest in the creatures we have brought back."

"I've no doubt I shall hear about them for weeks!" She looked at the canyons of his face and said, in the same humorously resigned tone, "Very well, I'll come along if you can't bear to have me out of your sight. But you'll have to go and get my wrap, because it is too cool to go outside without it."

Not making a graceful thing of it, Ainson left them. Pasztor cocked an eyebrow at Enid, and secured them a drink apiece.

"I don't know really whether I ought to have another, Mihaly. Wouldn't it be terrible if I got tipsy!"

"People do, you know. Look at Mrs. Friar over there. Now I've got you alone, Enid, instead of flirting with you as I have a mind to do, I have to ask you about your son, Aylmer. What is he doing now? Where is he?"

He detected her brief flush. She looked away from him as she spoke.

"Don't please, don't spoil the evening, Mihaly. It's so nice to have Bruce back. I know you think he's a terrible old monster, but he isn't really, not underneath."

"How is Aylmer?"

"He's in London. Apart from that, I don't know."

"You are too harsh with him."

"Please, Mihaly!"

"Bruce is too harsh with him. You know I say that as

an old friend, as well as Aylmer's godfather."

"He did something disgraceful, and his father turned him out of the house. They have never got on well together, as you know, and although I am terribly sorry about the boy, it is much more peaceful without having both of them to cope with." She looked up at him to add, "And don't go thinking I always take the line of least resistance, because I don't. For years I had a real battle with them."

"I never saw a face look less embattled. What did Aylmer do to bring this terrible edict down upon his head?"

"You must ask Bruce, if you're so keen to know."

"There was a girl involved?"

"Yes, it was over a girl. And here comes Bruce."

When the Master Explorer had settled the wrap about his wife's shoulders, Mihaly led them out of the hall by a side door. They walked along a carpeted corridor, downstairs, and out into the dusk. The zoo lay quiet, though one or two London starlings moved belatedly to bed among the trees, and from its heated pool a Rungsted's sauropod raised its neck to gaze in a dim wonder at their passage. Turning before they reached the Methane Mammal House, Pasztor led his companions to a new block constructed in the modern manner of sanded reinforced plastic blocks and strawed concrete with lead verticals. As they entered by a side door, lights came on.

Reinforced curving glass separated them from the two ETA's. The creatures turned about as the lights came on, to watch the humans. Ainson made a half-hearted gesture of recognition towards them; it produced no perceptible reaction.

"At least they have spacious accommodation," he said. "Does the public have to throng here all day, pressing its beastly noses to the glass?"

"The public will only be admitted to this block between

47

2.30 and 4 in the afternoon," Pasztor said, "In the mornings, experts will be here studying our visitors."

The visitors had an ample double cage, the two parts separated by a low door. At the back of one room was a wide low bed padded with a plastic foam. Troughs filled with food and water lined one of the other walls. The ETA's stood in the centre of the floor; they had already amassed a fair amount of dirt about them.

Three lizard-like animals scuttled across the floor and flung themselves on to the massive bodies of the ETA's. They scuttled for a fold of skin and disappeared. Ainson pointed towards them.

"You see that? Then they are still there. They look very like lizards. I believe there are four of them all together; they keep close to the extra-terrestrials. There were two of them accompanying the dying ETA we took aboard the *Mariestopes*. Probably they are synoecists or even symbionts. The fool of a captain heard of them from my reports and wanted them destroyed – said they might be dangerous parasites – but I stood out against him."

"Who was that? Edgar Bargerone?" Pasztor asked. "A brave man, not brilliant; he probably still clings to the geocentric conception of the universe."

"He wanted me to be communicating with these fellows before we touched Earth! He has no conception of the problems confronting us."

Enid, who had been watching the captives intently, looked up and asked, "Are you going to be able to communicate with them?"

"The question is not as simple as it would appear to a layman, my dear. I'll tell you all about it another time."

"For God's sake, Bruce, I'm not a child. Are you or aren't you going to be able to communicate with them?"

The Master Explorer tucked his hands into the hip flounces of his uniform and regarded his wife. When he spoke, it was smoulderingly, as a preacher from the elevation of a pulpit.

"With a quarter of a century's stellar exploration behind us, Enid, the nations of Earth – despite the fact that the total number of operational starships at any one time rarely exceeds a dozen – have managed to survey about three hundred roughly Earth-type planets. On those three hundred planets, Enid, they have sometimes found sentient life and sometimes not. But they have never found beings that could be regarded as having any more brain than a chimpanzee. Now we have discovered these creatures on Clementina, and we have our reasons for suspecting that they may possess an intelligence equivalent to man's – the main circumstantial reason being that they have an – er, machine capable of travelling between planets."

"Why make such a mystery of it, then?" Enid asked. "There are fairly simple tests devised for this situation; why not apply them? Do these creatures have a written script? Do they talk with each other? Do they observe a code between themselves? Are they able to repeat a simple demonstration or a set of gestures? Do they respond to simple mathematical concepts? What is their attitude towards human artifacts – and, of course, have they artifacts of their own? How do —"

" Yes, yes, my dear, we entirely take your point: there are tests to be applied. I was not idle on the voyage home; I applied the tests."

"Well, then, the results?"

"Conflicting. Conflicting in a way that suggests that the tests we applied were inefficient and insufficient – in a word, too steeped in anthropomorphism. And that is the point I was trying to make. Until we can define intelligence more nearly, we are not going to find it easy to begin communicating."

"At the same time," Pasztor supplemented, "you are

going to find it hard to define intelligence until you have succeeded in communicating."

Ainson brushed this aside with the gesture of a practical man cutting through sophisms.

"First we define intelligence. Is the little spider, *argyroneta aquatica*, intelligent because she can build a diving bell and thus live underwater? No. Very well, then these lumbering creatures may be no more intelligent because they can construct a spaceship. On the other hand, these creatures may be so highly intelligent, and the end-products of a civilization so ancient, that all the reasoning we conduct in our conscious minds, they conduct in their hereditary or subconscious minds leaving their conscious minds free for cogitation on matters – and indeed for forms of cogitation – beyond our understanding. If that is so, communication between our species may be for ever out of the question. Remember that one dictionary definition of intelligence is simply 'information received'; if we receive no information from them, and they none from us, then we are entitled to say these ETA's are unintelligent."

"This is all very puzzling to me," Enid said. "You make it sound so difficult now, yet in your letters you made it sound so simple. You said these creatures had come up and attempted to communicate with you in a series of grunts and whistles; you said they each possessed six excellent hands; you said they had arrived on what's it – on Clementina, by spaceship. Surely the situation is clear. They are intelligent; not simply with the limited intelligence of an animal, but intelligent enough to have produced a civilization and a language. The only problem is to translate their noises and whistles into English."

Ainson turned to the Director.

"You understand why it isn't so easy, don't you, Mihaly?"

"Well, I have read most of your reports, Bruce. I know these are mammals with respiratory systems and digestive

50

tracts much like ours, that they have brains with a similar weight ratio to our own, that possessing hands they would approach the universe with the same basic feeling we have that matter is there to be manipulated – no, frankly, Bruce, I can see that to learn their language or to get them to learn ours may be a difficult task, but I do feel you are overestimating the hazards of the case.''

"Do you? You wait till you've observed these fellows for a while. You'll feel differently. I tell you, Mihaly, I try to put myself in their place, and despite their disgusting habits I have managed to preserve sympathy towards them. But the only feeling I get – amid an ocean of frustration – is that they must, if they are intelligent at all, have a very different point of view to the universe from ours. Really, you'd imagine they were – they were —" he gestured at them, calm behind the glass – "holding themselves aloof from me."

"We shall have to see how the linguists get on," Pasztor said. "And Bryant Lattimore of USGN Flight Advice – he's a very forceful man – I think you'll like him – arrives from the States tomorrow. His views will be worth having." It was not the remark to please Bruce Ainson. He decided he had had enough of the subject.

"It's ten o'clock," he said. "Time Enid and I were shuttling home; you know I keep regular hours when I'm on Earth. We've enjoyed the celebrations, Mihaly. We shall see you at the end of the week."

They shook hands with returning cordiality. Provoked by one of the bursts of mischief that ensured he would never rise higher than his present sinecure, Sir Mihaly asked, "By the way, my friend, what was it Aylmer and the girl did that so conflicted with your point of view that you threw him out of your home?"

A tinge as of dusty brick mottled Bruce Ainson's throat and jowls.

"You'd better ask him yourself; he may see fit to gratify

your curiosity; I don't see him any more," he said stiffly. "We'll find our own way out."

The shuttle on the district line climbed upwards through a night punctuated by the city's orchestra of lights. It clung dizzily to its thread of rail. Enid closed her eyes and wished she had swallowed an Antivom before they boarded; she was not a good traveller.

"A tubby for your thoughts," her husband said.

"I wasn't thinking, Bruce."

After a silence, Ainson said. "What were you and Mihaly talking about while I went to get your wrap?"

"I don't remember. Trivialities. Why do you ask that?"

"How much did you see of him while I was away?"

She sighed, and the noise of the air flowing past the cab drowned the small sound she made.

"You always ask me that, Bruce, after each trip. Now stop being jealous or you'll give me ideas; Mihaly is very sweet but he means nothing to me."

High above outer London, the district shuttle decanted them on to the great curled lip of the Outflank Ring. Their section of the newly-built structure was crowded, so that they preserved silence as they whirled towards the non-stop lane that would take them home. But once on the monobus, their silence continued to cling. Neither felt comfortable in the other's lack of speech, fearing unknown thought. Enid spoke first.

"Well, I'm glad success has come to you at last, Bruce. We must have a party. I'm very proud of you, you know!"

He patted her hand and smiled at her forgivingly, as one might to a child.

"There won't be time for parties, I'm afraid. This is when the real work begins. I shall have to be round at the zoo every day, advising the research teams. They can't very well do without me, you know."

She stared ahead of her. She was not really disappointed;

she should have expected the answer she got. And even then, instead of showing anger, she found herself trying to be friendly with him, asking one of her silly little searched-for questions.

"I suppose you are hoping very much that we can learn to talk to these creatures?"

"The government seems less excited than I had hoped. Of course I know there is this wretched war on. . . . Eventually there may be points emerging that prove of more importance than the language factor."

She recognized a vagueness in his phraseology he used when there was something he was unsure of.

"What sort of points?"

He stared into the rushing night.

"The wounded ETA showed a great resistance to dying. When they dissected it on the *Mariestopes*, they cut it almost into chunks before it died. These things have a phenomenal resistance to pain. They don't feel pain. They don't . . . feel pain! Think of it. It's all in the reports, buried in tables and written up technically – I've no patience with it any longer. But one day someone's going to see the importance of those facts."

Again she felt his silence fall like a stone from his lips as he looked past her through the window.

"You saw this creature being cut up?"

"Of course I did."

She thought about all the things that men did and bore with apparent ease.

"Can you imagine it?" Ainson said. "Never to feel any pain, physical or mental. . . ."

They were sinking down to the local traffic level. His melancholy gaze rested on the darkness that concealed their home.

"What a boon to mankind!" he exclaimed.

After the Ainsons had gone, Sir Mihaly Pasztor stood

where he was, in a vacuity that occasionally merged into thought. He began to pace up and down, watched by the eyes of the two alien beings beyond the glass. Their glance finally slowed him; he came to rest on the balls of his feet, balancing, swaying gently, regarding them with folded arms, and finally addressing them.

"My dear charges, I understand the problem, and without having met you before, I do to a certain limited extent also understand you. Above all I understand that up until now you have only been faced with a limited type of human mind. I know spacemen, my bag-bellied friends, for I was a spaceman myself, and I know how the long dark years attract and mould an inflexible mind. You have been faced with men without the human touch, men without finer perceptions, men without the gift of empathy, men who do not readily excuse and understand because they have no knowledge of the diversity of human habits, men who because they have no insight into themselves are denied insight into others.

"In short, my dear and dung-stained charges, if you are civilized, then you need to be confronted by a properly civilized man. If you are more than animal, then it should not be too long before we understand each other. After that will be time for words to grow between us."

One of the ETA's deretracted his limbs, rose, and came over to the glass. Sir Mihaly Pasztor took it as an omen.

Going round to the back of the enclosure, he entered a small anteroom to the actual cage. Pressing a button, he activated the part of the floor on which he stood; it moved forward into the cage, carrying before it a low barrier, so that the Director looked rather like a prisoner entering court in a knee-high dock. The mechanism stopped. He and the ETA's were now face to face, although a button by Pasztor's right hand ensured that he could withdraw himself immediately, should danger threaten.

The ETA's made thin whistles and huddled together.

Their smell, while far from being as repugnant as might have been expected, was certainly very noticeable. Mihaly wrinkled his nose.

"To our way of thought," he said, "civilization is reckoned as the distance man has placed between himself and his excreta."

One of the ETA's extended a limb and scratched itself.

"We have no civilizations on Earth that are not firmly founded on an alphabet. Even the aborigine sketches his fears and hopes on the rocks. But do you have fears and hopes?"

The limb, having scratched, retracted, leaving the palm of the hand merely as a six-pointed pattern in the flesh.

"It is impossible to imagine a creature larger than a flea without fears and hopes, or some such equivalent structure based on pain stimuli. Good feelings and bad feelings: they get us through life, they are our experiences of the external world. Yet if I understand the report on the autopsy of one of your late friends, you experience no pain. How radically that must modify your experience of the external world."

One of the lizard creatures appeared. It scuttled along its host's back and applied its little twinkling nose to a fold of skin. It became motionless, and all but invisible.

"And indeed, what is the external world? Since we can only know it through our senses, we can never know it undiluted; we can only know it as external-world-plus-senses. What is a street? To a small boy, a whole world of mystery. To a military strategist, a series of strong points and exposed positions; to a lover, his beloved's dwelling place; to a prostitute, her place of business; to an urban historian, a series of watermarks in time; to an architect, a treaty drawn between art and necessity; to a painter, an adventure in perspective and tone; to a traveller, the location of drink and a warm bed; to the oldest inhabitant, a monument to his past follies, hopes, and hearts; to the

55

motorist —

"How then do our external worlds, yours and mine, my enigmatic kine, clash or chine? Are we not going to find that somewhat difficult to discover until we have succeeded in speaking to each other beyond a list of nouns and needs? Or do you, with our Master Explorer, prefer the proposition reversed: do we have to grasp the nature of at least your external environment before we can parley?

"And have I not suddenly deviated into sense, sows? For might it not be that you two forlorn creatures are merely hostages to the larger question. Perhaps we shall never communicate with either of the pair of you. But you are a sign that somewhere – perhaps not too many light years from Clementina – is a planet full of your kind. If we went *there*, if we caught you in your natural haunts, then we would understand so much more about you, would see far more precisely what we should be trying to parley about. We not only need linguists here; we need a couple of starships searching the worlds near Clementina. I must make the point to Lattimore."

The ETA's did nothing.

"I warn you, man is a very persistent creature. If the external world won't come to him, he will go to the external world. If you have vocabularies to shed, prepare to shed them now."

Their eyes had closed.

"Have you lapsed into unconsciousness or prayer? The latter would be wiser, now that you are in the hands of man."

Philosophizing was not all that went on that first night that *Mariestopes* rested her terrigenous bulk on Earth; there was also house-breaking.

Not that Rodney Walthamstone could help it, as his defence explained when the case came up. It was a compulsion of a not unusual sort in these modern days, when every other month saw the return of ships which had probed into the very depths of the cosmos. Ordinary mortals sailed on those terrible – and he used the word without intending hyperbole – those terrible voyages; mortals, m'lud, like Rodney Walthamstone, upon whom space could not but have an overwhelming effect. This was well known, and had been designated Bestar's Syndrome ten years ago (named after the celebrated psychodynamician, m'lud).

Out in the cosmos, all the fundamental symbols and furnishings of man's minds were lacking, brutally lacking. One did not have to agree with the French philosopher Deutch that cosmos and mind were the two opposed poles of the magnet of entirety to realize that space travel imposed a great strain on any man, and that he might return to Earth with a hunger for normality that could not be satisfied through legal channels. Granted that be so, then it was this law and not the mind of man that should be altered; man had gone out into the infinite starry depths: it was up to the law to make itself somewhat less earthbound (laughter).

What symbol had more powerful hold over man's mind than a house, that symbol of home, of shelter from the hostile world, of civilization itself? So in this case of housebreaking, unfortunate though it was that the house owner had been coshed, the court should see that the not unheroic accused had merely been searching for a symbol. Of course, he admitted freely to having been slightly under the influence of drink at the same time, but Bestar's Syndrome allowed —

The judge, allowing that the defence had a point, said he was nevertheless tired of space ratings who came back to Earth and treated England as if it were a bit of the undeveloped cosmos. Thirty days behind bars might convince the prisoner that there was a considerable difference between the two.

The court adjourned for lunch, and a Miss Florence Walthamstone was led weeping from the court into the nearest public house.

"Hank, honey, you aren't really going to join the Space Corps, are you? You aren't going off into space again, are you?"

"I *told* you, honey, just on a Flight-by-Flight arrangement, like I had in the Exploration Corps."

"I'll never understand you men, not if I live to be a thousand. What's *out* there, that attracts you? What do you get out of it?"

"Hell, it's a way of earning your living. Better than an office job, isn't it? I'm a brainy guy, honey, you don't seem to realize, passed all my exams, but there's so much competition here in America."

"But what do you *get* out of it, that's what I want to know."

"I told you, I may wind up captain. Now how about letting the subject rest for a bit, hey?"

"I didn't want to talk about it."

"You didn't? Well, who do you think did, then? Sometimes I think you and me just don't talk the same language."

"Darling. Darling! Darling, don't you think it's time we got up now?"

"Mmm?"

"It's ten o'clock, darling."

"Mmm. Early yet."

"I'm hungry."

"I was dreaming about you, Gussie."

"We were going to get the eleven o'clock ferry across to Hong Kong, remember? You were going to sketch today, remember?"

"Mmm. Kiss me again, darling."

"Mmm. Darling."

CHAPTER SIX

HEAD Keeper was a sparse grey man who had recently taken to brushing his hair so that it showed under each side of his peaked cap. He had worked under Pasztor long ago – many moons before he had had trouble in walking downstairs in the morning – far below the icy cliffs of the Ross Ice Shelf. His name, as it happened, was Ross, Ian Edward Tinghe Ross, and he gave Bruce Ainson a smart salute as the explorer came up.

"Morning, Ross. How's everything this morning? I'm late."

"Big conference this morning, sir. They've only just started. Sir Mihaly is in there, of course, and the three linguists – Dr. Bodley Temple and his two associates – and a statistician, I forget his name, little man with a warty neck, you can't miss him, and a lady – a scientist, I believe – and that Oxford philosopher again, Roger Wittgenbacher, and our American friend, Lattimore, and the novelist, Gerald Bone, and who else?"

"Good Lord, that makes about a dozen! What's Gerald Bone doing here?"

"He's a friend of Sir Mihaly's, as I understand it, sir. I thought he looked a very nice man. My own reading tastes are on the more serious side, and so I don't often read any novels, but now and again when I haven't been well – particularly when I had that spot of bronchitis last winter, if you remember – I have dipped into one or two better novels, and I must say that I was very impressed by Mr. Bone's *Many Are The Few*. The hero had had a nervous breakdown —"

"Yes, I do recall the plot, Ross, thank you. And how are our two ETA's?"

"Quite honestly, sir, I reckon they're dying of boredom, and who's to blame them!"

When Ainson entered the study room that lay behind the ETA's cage, it was to find the conference in session. Counting heads as they nodded to him in recognition, he amassed a total of fourteen males and one female. Although they were unalike in appearance, there was a feeling of something shared about them: perhaps an air of authority.

This air was most noticeable about Mrs. Warhoon, if only because she was on her feet and in full spate when Ainson arrived. Mrs. Hilary Warhoon was the lady that Head Keeper Ross had referred to. Though only in her mid-forties, she was well-known as a leading cosmoclectic, the new philosophico-scientific profession that attempted to sort the wheat from the chaff in the rapidly accumulating pile of facts and theories which represented Earth's main import from space. Ainson looked at her with approval. To think she should be married to some dried old stick of a banker she could not tolerate! She was a fine figure of a woman, fashionable enough to be wearing one of the new chandelier style suits with pendants at bust, hip, and thigh level; the appeal of her face, serious though her prevalent expression might be, was not purely intellectual; while Ainson knew for a fact that she could out-argue even old Wittgenbacher, Oxford's professional philosopher and technivision pundit. In fact, Ainson could not help comparing her with his wife, to Enid's disadvantage. One, of course, would never dream of indicating one's inner feelings to her, poor thing, or to anyone else, but really Enid was a poor specimen; she should have married a shopkeeper in a busy country town. Banbury. Diss. East Dereham. Yes, that was about it. . . .

". . . feel that we have made progress this week, despite several handicaps inherent in the situation, most of them stemming – as I think the Director was the first to point out – from the fact that we have no background to the lifeform to use as a point of reference." Mrs. Warhoon's voice was pleasantly staccato. It scattered Ainson's thoughts and made him concentrate on what she was saying; if Enid had been a bit more prompt with the breakfast, he might have got here in time to hear the beginning of her speech. "My colleague, Mr. Borroughs, and I have now examined the space vehicle found on Clementina. While we are not qualified to give a technical report on it – you will be getting several technical reports on it from other sources in any case – we both were convinced that it was a vehicle developed for, if not by, the captive lifeform. You will recall that eight of the lifeforms were discovered close to the vehicle; and the body of a dead one was disinterred within the vehicle itself; nine bunks, or niches that by their shape and size are intended to serve as bunks, are observable within the vehicle. Because these bunks run in the direction we think of as vertical rather than horizontally, and are separated by what we now know to be fuel lines, they have not previously been recognized as bunks.

"Here it is appropriate to mention another trouble that we come up against continually. We do not know what is evidence and what is not.

"For instance, we now have to ask ourselves, supposing we consider it established that the lifeform has developed space travel: can space travel be regarded as *a priori* proof of superior intelligence?"

"That is the most penetrating question I have heard

61

asked in the last decade," said Wittgenbacher, nodding his head six times with the frightening assurance of a clockwork doll. "If it were posed to the masses, they would give you but one answer, or should I rather say that their many answers would take but one form. They would render an affirmative. We who are here may reckon ourselves more enlightened and would perhaps choose as a more valid example of superior intelligence the works of the analytical philosophers, where logic flows unconfused with emotion. But the masses – and who perhaps amongst us in the final analysis is to gainsay them? – would, if I may employ a colloquialism, plump for a product in which the hands as well as the mind had been employed. I do not doubt that among such a category of products the spaceship would appear to them the most outstanding."

"I'd go along with them," said Lattimore. He sat next to Pasztor, sucking the frame of his spectacles and listening intently.

"I might even accompany them myself," chuckled Wittgenbacher, with more mechanical nods. "But this does raise another question. Suppose that, having granted this lifeform, so unaesthetically unhygienic in many of its habits, superior intelligence; suppose we later discover its planet of origin, and then perceive that its – um, its space-going ability is as much governed by instinctual behaviour as is the ocean-going ability of our northern fur-seals. Perhaps you will correct me if I am in error, Sir Mihaly, but I believe that the *Arctocephalus ursinus*, the bear seal, makes a winter migration of many thousands of miles from the Bering Sea down to the shores of Mexico, where I have seen them myself when swimming in the Gulf of California.

"If we find this to be so, then not only shall we be in error in presuming superior intelligence in our friends, but we shall have to ask ourselves this: is it not possible that our own space travel is equally the outcome of instinctual behaviour, and – much as the fur-seal may imagine on his swim south that his travel is prompted by his own will – may we not be pushed by an unglimpsed purpose beyond our own?"

Three reporters at the back of the room scribed busily, ensuring that tomorrow's *Times*, recording the longueurs of the conference, would pinpoint this highlight in a head-line reading:

SPACE TRAVEL: MAN'S MIGRATORY PATTERN?

Gerald Bone stood up. The novelist's face had lit at the new thought like a child's at sight of a new toy.

"Do I understand you, Professor Wittgenbacher, to imply that we – that our much-vaunted intelligence, the one thing that most clearly distinguishes us from the animals, may really be no more than a blind compulsion driving us in its own directions rather than in ours?"

"Why not? For all our pretensions to the arts and the humanities, our race ever since the Renaissance at least has directed its main efforts towards the twin goals of expanding its numbers and expanding outwards." Having got the bit between his teeth, the old philosopher was not going to stop there. "In fact you may liken our leaders to the queen bee who prepares her hive to swarm and does not know why she does it. We swarm into space and do not know why we do it. Something drives —"

But he was not going to get away with it. Lattimore was the first to vent a hearty "Nonsense", and Dr. Bodley Temple and his assistants made unsavoury noises of dis-sent. All round the room, the professor was given the cultural catcall.

"Preposterous theory —"

"Economic possibilities inherent in —"

"Even a techni audience would hardly —"

"I suppose the colonization of other planets —"

"One just cannot dismiss the diciplines of science —"

"Order, please," called the Director.

In the following lull, Gerald Bone called another question to Wittgenbacher, "Then where shall we find true intellect?"

"Perhaps when we run up against our gods," Wittgenbacher replied, not at all put out by the heated atmosphere about him.

"We will have the linguistic report now," Pasztor said sharply, and Dr. Bodley Temple rose, rested his right leg on the chair in front of him, rested his right elbow on his knee, so that he leant forward with an appearance of eagerness, and did not budge from that position until he had finished talking. He was a small stocky man with a screw of grey hair rising from the middle of his forehead and a pugnacious expression. He had the reputation of being a sound and imaginative scholar, and offset it with some of the nattiest waistcoats in London University. His present one, negotiating a considerable stretch of abdomen, was of antique brocade with a pattern of Purple Emperor butterflies chasing themselves about the buttons.

"You all know what the job of my team is," he said, in a voice that Arnold Bennett would have recognized a century back as having sprung from the Five Towns. "We're trying to learn the alien tongue without knowing if they have one, because that's the only way there is to find out. We have made some progress, as my colleague Wilfred Brebner here will demonstrate in a moment.

"First, I'll make a few general remarks. Our visitors, these fat chaps from Clementina, don't understand what writing is. They have no script. That doesn't mean anything with regard to their language – many African negro languages were only reduced to writing by white missionaries. Efik and Yoruba were two such languages of the Sudanic language group; almost unused languages now, I'd say.

" I tell you all this, my friends, because until I get a better idea, I'm treating these aliens as a couple of

Africans. It may bring results. It's more positive than treating them as animals – you may recall that the first white explorers in Africa thought the negroes were gorillas – and it ensures that if we find they do have a language, then we won't make the mistake of expecting it to follow anything like a Romance pattern.

"I am certain that our fat friends have a language – and you gents of the Press can quote me there, if you like. You've only got to listen to them snorting together. And it isn't all snorts. We've now analysed it from tapes and have sorted out five hundred different sounds. Though it may be that many of these sounds are the same sound delivered at a different pitch. You may know that there are terrestrial linguistic systems such as – er, Siamese and Cantonese which employ six acoustic pitches. And we can expect many more pitches with these fellows, who obviously range very freely over the sound spectrum.

"The human ear is deaf to vibrations of frequency greater than somewhere about 24,000 a second. We have found that these chaps can go twice that, just as a terrestrial bat or a Rungstedian cat can. So one problem is that if we are to converse with them, we must get them to stay within our wavelength. For all we know, that may mean they would have to invent a sort of pidgin language that we could understand."

"I protest," said the statistician, who until now had been content to do little but run his tongue round his teeth. "You are now inferring, surely, that we are inferior to them."

"I'm saying nothing of the kind. I'm saying that their range of sound is very much greater than ours. Now, Mr. Brebner here is going to give us a few of the phonemes that we have provisionally identified."

Mr. Brebner rose and stood swaying beside the stocky figure of Bodley Temple. He was in his mid-twenties, a slight figure with pale yellow hair, wearing a light grey suit with the hood down. His face was suffused a delicate flame colour with the embarrassment of confronting his audience, but he spoke up well.

"The dissections on the dead aliens have told us quite a lot about their anatomy," he said. "If you have read the rather lengthy report, you will know that our friends have three distinct classes of apertures through which they produce their characteristic noises. All these noises appear to contribute to their language, or we assume they do, just as we assume they have a language.

"First, they have in one of their heads a mouth, to which is linked a scent organ. Although this mouth is used for breathing, its main function is feeding and making what we term the oral sounds.

"Secondly, our friends have six breathing vents, three on either side of their body, and situated above their six limbs. At present we refer to these as the nostrils. They are labiate apertures and although unconnected to any vocal chords – as is the mouth – these nostrils produce a wide range of sounds.

"Thirdly, our friends also produce a variety of controlled sound through the rectum situated in their second head.

"Their form of speech consists of sound transmitted through all these apertures, either in turn, or any two together, or all three classes together. or all eight apertures together. You will see then that the few sounds I am now going to give you as examples are limited to the less complex ones. Tape recordings of the whole range are of course available, but are not in a very manageable form as yet.

"The first word is *nnnnorrrr*-INK."

To pronounce this word, Wilfred Brebner ran a light snore over the front of his throat and chased it with the little squeak represented here as "ink". (All printed forms of the alien language used throughout this book are

66

similarly to be treated as mere approximations.)

Brebner continued with his exposition.

"*Nnnnorrrr*-INK is the word we have obtained several times in various contexts. Dr. Bodley Temple recorded it first last Saturday, when he brought our friends a fresh cabbage. We obtained it a second time on Saturday when I took out a packet of chewing plastic and gave pieces to Dr. Temple and to Mike. We did not hear it again till Tuesday afternoon, when it was pronounced in a situation when food was not present. Chief Keeper Ross had entered the cage where we were to see if we needed anything, and both creatures made the sound at the same time. We then noted that the word might have a negative connotation, since they had refused the cabbage, and had not been offered the chew – which they would presume to be food – and might be supposed not to like Ross, who disturbs them when he cleans out their cage. Yesterday, however, Ross brought them a bucket of river mud, which they like, and then we recorded *nnnnorrrr*-INK again, several times in five minutes. So we think at present that it refers to some variety of human activity: appearing bearing something, shall we say. The meaning will be fined down considerably as we go along. From this example you can see the process of elimination we go through with every sound.

"The bucket of river mud also brought forth another word we can recognize. This sounds like WHIP-*bwut-bwip* (a small whistle followed by two pouting labials). We have also heard it when grapefruit has been accepted, when porridge with sliced banana in – a dish over which they show some enthusiasm – has been accepted, and when Mike and I have been leaving in the evening. We take it therefore to be a sign of approval.

"We also think we have a sign of disapproval, although we have only heard it twice. Once it was accompanied by a gesture of disapproval, when an under-keeper caught one of our friends on the snout with a jet of water from a hose. On the other occasion, we had offered them fish, some cooked, some raw. As you are aware, they seem to be vegetarians. The sound was —"

Brebner glanced apologetically at Mrs. Warhoon as he blew a series of damp farts with his mouth, culminating with an open-mouthed groan.

"Bbbp-bbbp-bbbp-bbbp-aaaah."

"It certainly sounds like disapproval," Temple said.

Before the ripple of amusement died, one of the reporters said, "Dr. Temple, is this all you have to offer in the way of progress?"

"You have been given a rough guide to what we are doing."

"But you don't seem to have a single one of their words definitely. Why couldn't you tackle what any layman would think would be the first steps, like getting them to count, and to name parts of their bodies and yours? Then at least you have something to begin on, rather than a few abstracts like 'Appearing carrying something'."

Temple looked down at the Purple Emperors on his waistcoat, munched his lips, and then said, "Young man, a layman might indeed think those were the first steps. But my answer to that layman and to you is that such a catalogue is only possible if the enemy – the alien is prepared to open up a conversation. These two buggers – I beg your pardon, madam – these two fellows have no interest in communicating with us."

"Why don't you get a computer on the job?"

"Your questions grow more foolish. You need common-sense on a job like this. What damned good would a computer be? It can't think, nor can it differentiate between two almost identical phonemes for us. All we need is time. You can't imagine – nor can your hypothetical layman – the difficulties that beset us, mainly because we are having to think in a realm where man has not had to think before.

68

Ask yourself this: what *is* language? And the answer is, human speech. Therefore we aren't just doing research, we are inventing something new: non-human speech."

The reporter nodded glumly, Dr. Temple huffed and puffed and sat down, Lattimore rose. He perched his spectacles on the end of his nose and clasped his hands behind his back.

"As you know, Doctor, I'm new around here, so I hope you'll appreciate I ask my questions in all innocence. My position is this. I'm a sceptic. I know that we have investigated only three hundred planets in this universe, and I know that leaves a tidy few million to go, but I still hold that three hundred is a fair sampling. None of them have yielded any form of life half as intelligent as my Siamese cat. This suggests to me that man is unique in the universe."

"It should be no stronger than a suggestion," Temple said.

"Nor is it. Now, I don't give a row of pins if there is no other form of intelligent life in the universe; man has always been on his own, and that won't worry him. On the other hand, if some other intelligent form of human turns up elsewhere, then I'll welcome it as readily as the next man – provided it behaves itself.

"What sticks in my gullet is when someone brings back this couple of overgrown hogs that wallow in their own filth in a way no self-respecting Earth pig would do, given the option, and insists that we try and prove that they are intelligent people! It's just crazy. You yourself said that these hogs show no interest in trying to communicate with us. Very well, then, isn't that a sign that they have no intelligence? Who in all this room can honestly say they would want these hogs in their own house?"

Uproar broke out again. Everyone turned and argued, not merely with Lattimore, but with each other. Finally it was Mrs. Warhoon's voice that rode over the rumpus.

"I have a great deal of sympathy with your position, Mr. Lattimore, and I am very glad you have consented to come down and sit in on our meeting. But the brief answer to you is that, as life takes a multitude of different forms, so we should expect intelligence to take differing forms. We cannot conceive a differing form of intelligence. We only know that it would widen the boundaries of our thought and understanding in a way that nothing else could. Therefore, when we think we have found such intelligence, we must make sure, even if the effort takes us years."

"That is part of my point, madam," Lattimore said. "If intelligence were there, it would not take us years to detect. We should recognize it right away, even if it came disguised as a turnip."

"How do you account for the space ship on Clementina?" Gerald Bone asked.

"I don't have to account for it! These big hogs should be able to account for it. If they built it, then why don't they draw pictures of it when they're given pencils and paper?"

"Because they travel in it doesn't mean to say they built it."

"Can you imagine the lowest dumbest rating on an Earth cruiser getting captured by aliens and then being unable to draw a picture of his ship when they brought him pencil and paper?"

Brebner asked, "And their language, how do you account for that?"

"I enjoyed your animal imitations, Mr. Brebner," Lattimore said good-humouredly. "But frankly, I converse more readily with my cat than you do with those two hogs."

Ainson spoke for the first time. He spoke sharply, annoyed that a mere interloper should be belittling his discovery.

"This is all very well, Mr. Lattimore, but you are dismissing too much too easily. We know the ETA's have certain habits that are unpleasant by our standards. But they don't behave together like animals; they provide companionship for each other. They converse. And the spaceship is there, whatever you may say."

"Maybe the spaceship is there. But what is the connection between the hogs and it? We don't know. They may well be just the livestock that the real space travellers took along for food. I don't know; but you don't know either, and you are avoiding the obvious explanation. Frankly, if I were in charge of this operation, I'd pass a hefty vote of censure on the captain of the *Mariestopes* and more particularly on his Master Explorer for carrying out such a sloppy piece of investigation on the spot."

At this, there was a sort of ominous and uneasy groundswell about the room. Only the reporters began to look a little happier. Sir Mihaly leant forward and explained to Lattimore who Ainson was. Lattimore pulled a long face.

"Mr. Explorer Ainson, I fear I owe you an apology for having failed to recognize you. If you'd been here before the meeting began, we could have been introduced."

"Unfortunately, this morning my wife —"

"But I must absolutely stick to what I said. The report on what happened on Clementina is pathetic in its amateurishness. Your stipulated week's reconnoitre of the planet was expired when you found these animals beside the spaceship, and rather than depart from schedule you just shot up the majority of them, took a few technishots of the scene, and blasted off. This ship, for all you know, may have been the equivalent of a cattle truck, with the cattle out to wallow, while two miles away in another valley was the real ship, with real bipeds like us, people – just like Mrs. Warhoon says – that we'd give our eyes and eye teeth to communicate with, and vice versa, you can be sure.

71

"No, I'm sorry, Mr. Ainson, but your committees here are more bogged down than they care to admit, simply because of bad field work on your part."

Ainson had grown very red. Something ghastly had happened in the room. The feeling had gone against him. Everyone – he knew it without looking at them – everyone was sitting in silent approval of what Lattimore said.

"Any idiot can be wise after the event," he said. "You seem to fail to realize how unprecedented it all was. I —"

"I do realize how unprecedented it all was. I'm saying that it was unprecedented, and that therefore you should have been more thorough. Believe me, Mr. Ainson, I've read photostats of the report on the expedition and I've scrutinized the photographs that were taken, and I have the impression that the whole thing was conducted more like a big game hunt than an official expedition paid for with public money."

"I was not responsible for the shooting of the six ETA's. A patrol ran into them, coming back to the ship late. It went to investigate the aliens, they attacked and were shot in self-defence. You should re-read the reports."

"These hogs show no sign of being vicious. I don't believe that they attacked the patrol. I think they were trying to run away."

Ainson looked about for help.

"I appeal to you, Mrs. Warhoon, is it reasonable to try and guess how these aliens behaved in their free state from a glance at their apathetic behaviour in captivity?"

Mrs. Warhoon had formed an immediate admiration for Bryant Lattimore; she liked a strong man.

"What other means have we for judging their behaviour?" she asked.

"You have the reports, that's what. There is a full account there for you to study."

Lattimore returned to the attack.

"What we have in the reports, Mr. Ainson, is a sum-

72

mary of what the leader of the patrol told you. Is he a reliable man?"

"Reliable? Yes, he is reliable enough. There is a war on in this country, you know, Mr. Lattimore, and we can't always choose the men we want."

"I see. And what was this man's name?"

And indeed what was his name? Young, beefy, rather sullen. Not a bad fellow. Horton? Halter? In a calmer atmosphere he would remember at once. Controlling his voice, Ainson said, "You will find his name in the written report."

"All right, all right, Mr. Ainson. Obviously you have your answers. What I'm saying is that you should have returned with a lot more answers. You see you are something of a keyman here, aren't you? You're the Master Explorer. You were trained up to just this situation. I'd say you have made it very difficult for all of us by producing inadequate or even conflicting data."

Lattimore sat down, leaving Ainson standing.

"The nature of the data is to be conflicting," Ainson said. "Your job is to make sense of it, not to reject it. Nobody is to blame. If you have any complaints, then they must be forwarded to Captain Bargerone. Captain Bargerone was in charge of the whole thing, not I. Oh, and Quilter was the name of the fellow in charge of the patrol. I've just remembered."

Gerald Bone spoke without rising.

"As you know, I'm a novelist, Mr. Ainson. Perhaps in this distinguished company I should say 'only a novelist'. But one thing has worried me about your part in this.

"Mr. Lattimore says that you should have returned from Clementina with more answers than you did. However that may be, it does seem to me that you have returned with a few assumptions which, because they have come from you, have been accepted all round without challenge as fact."

With dry mouth, Ainson waited for what was to come. Again he was aware that everyone was listening with a sort of predatory eagerness.

"We know that these ETA's were found by a river on Clementina. Everyone also seems to accept that they are not natives of that planet. As far as I can see, this notion began with you. Is that so?"

The question was a relief. This Ainson could answer.

"The notion did begin with me, Mr. Bone, though I would call it a conclusion rather than a notion. I can explain it easily, even to a layman. These ETA's belonged to the ship; be quite clear about that. Their excreta was caked all over the inside of it – a computed thirty days' accumulation of it. As additional evidence, the ship was clearly built in their image."

"The *Mariestopes*, you might say, is built in the image of the common dolphin. It proves nothing about the shape of the engineers who designed it."

"Please be courteous enough to hear me out. We found no other mammalian type life of 12B – Clementina, as it is now called. We found no animal life larger than a two-inch tail-less lizard and no insect life larger than a type of bee as big as a common shrew. In a week, with stratospheric surveys day and night, you cover a planet pretty thoroughly from pole to equator. Excluding the fish in the seas, we discovered that Clementina had no animal life worth mentioning – except these big creatures that turn the scales at twenty Earth stones. And they were together in one group by the spaceship. Clearly it is an absurdity to suppose them to be natives."

"You found them beside a river. Why should they not be an aquatic animal, possibly one that spends most of its time at sea?"

Ainson opened and shut his mouth. "Sir Mihaly, this discussion naturally raises points that a layman can hardly be expected ... I mean, no purpose is served. ..."

74

"Quite so," agreed Pasztor. "All the same, I think Gerald has an interesting point. Do you feel we can definitely rule out the possibility that these fellows are aquatic?"

"As I've said, they came from the spaceship. That was absolutely conclusive, you have my word for it as the man on the spot." As he spoke, Ainson's eye went belligerently over the group; when it met Lattimore's eye, Lattimore spoke.

"I would say they had the lines of a marine animal – speaking purely as a layman, of course."

"Perhaps they are aquatic on their own planet, but that has no bearing on what they were doing on Clementina," Ainson said. "Whatever you say, their spaceship is a spaceship, and consequently we have intelligence on our hands."

Mihaly came to his rescue then, and called for the next report, but it was obvious that a vote of no confidence had been passed on Master Explorer Ainson.

CHAPTER SEVEN

THE sun, as its inalienable custom was, went to bed at sunset. At the same time, Sir Mihaly Pasztor put on a dinner jacket and went to meet the guests he had invited to dine at his flat.

This was a month after the dismal meeting at the zoo

when Bruce Ainson had received the intellectual equivalent of a flea in his ear.

Since then, the situation could not be said to have improved. Dr. Bodley Temple had accumulated an impressive hoard of alien phonemes, none of which had a certain English equivalent. Lattimore had amplified in print the views he had expressed at the meeting. Gerald Bone – traitorously, thought Pasztor – had done a malicious little skit on the meeting for *Punch*.

These were but pin-pricks. The fact was, there was no progress being made. There was no progress being made chiefly because the aliens, imprisoned in their hygienic cell, showed no interest in the humans, nor any wish to co-operate in any of the stunts the humans devised. This disobliging attitude had its effect on the research team trying to deal with them; their increasing moroseness became increasingly punctuated with bouts of self-pitying oration, as if, like a Communist millionaire, they felt impelled to explain a position of some delicacy.

The general public, too, reacted adversely to the alien cold shoulder. The intelligent man in the street could have appreciated an intelligent alien, no matter what his shape, as a new distraction to compete with the world series, the grim news from Charon, where Brazil seemed to be winning the war, or the leaping taxes that were a natural concomitant to both war and TP travel. Gradually the queues that stood all day to see the aliens in the afternoon dwindled away (after all, they didn't move about much, and they looked not so very different from terrestrial hippos, and you weren't allowed to throw nuts at them in case it turned out they really lived in skyscrapers back home) and went back to their old routine of watching instead the Pinfold III primaritals, which indulged in a form of group intercourse every hour on the hour.

Pasztor was, as it happened, thinking of intercourse as he ushered his guest, Mrs. Hilary Warhoon, into his modest dining-closet; or if not thinking of it, reviewing with a whimsical smile at his own weaknesses the fantasies with which he had indulged himself half an hour before Mrs. Warhoon's arrival. But no, she was not quite enchanting enough, and Mr. Warhoon by repute was too powerful and spiteful, and anyhow Sir Mihaly no longer had the zest necessary to carry off one of those illicit affairs – even though "illicit" was one of the more alluring words in the English language.

She sat down at the table and sighed.

"It's wonderful to relax. I've had a vile day."

"Busy?"

"I've made work. But I've accomplished nothing. And I'm oppressed by a sense of failure."

"You, Hilary? You are far from being a failure."

"I was thinking of it less in a personal than in a general or racial sense. Do you want me to elaborate? I'd like to elaborate."

He held up his hands in playful protest.

"My idea of civilized intercourse is not to repress but to bring forth, to elaborate. I have never been other than interested in what you have to say."

There were three globular table ovens standing on the table. As she began to speak, he opened the refrigerated drawers on his right and began to put their contents into the ovens to cook: Fera de Travers, the salmon of Lake Geneva, to begin with, to be followed by eland steaks flown that morning from the farms of Kenya with, to add a touch of the exotic, fingerlips, the Venusian asparagus.

"When I say I'm oppressed by a general failure," Mrs. Warhoon said, attacking a dry sherry, "I'm fully aware that it sounds rather pretentious. 'Who am I among so many?', as Shaw once said in a different context. It's the old problems of definitions, with which the aliens have confronted us in dramatic new guise. Perhaps we cannot converse with them until we have decided for ourselves what constitutes civilization. Don't raise that suave eyebrow at me, Mihaly; I know civilization does not consist of lying indolent in one's own droppings – though it's possible that if we had a guru here he would tell us it did.

"When you take any one quality by which we measure civilization, you will find it missing from various cultures. Take the whole question of crime. For over a century, we have recognized crime as a symptom of sickness or unhappiness. Once we recognized that in practice as well as theory, crime statistics dropped dramatically for the first time. But in many periods of high civilization, life imprisonment was customary, heads fell like petals. Certainly kindness or understanding or mercy are not signs of civilization, any more than war and murder are signs of the lack of it.

"As for the arts that we rightly cherish, they were all practised by prehistoric man."

"This argument is familiar to me from my undergraduate days," Sir Mihaly said, as he served the salmon. "Yet still we cook our food and eat according to rules with carefully wrought utensils." He poured some wine. "Still we choose our vintages and exercise our judgments and our prejudices over that choice." He offered her a basket full of warm crisp rolls. "Still we sit together, male and female, and merely converse."

"I'm not denying, Mihaly, that you keep a good table, or that you have failed as yet to throw me on the floor. But this meal – and I cast no aspersions – is now an anachronism, and strongly disapproved of by a government pushing the new poison-free man-made foods and drinks. Besides, this lovely meal is the end product of a number of factors that have only a nodding acquaintance with true civility. I mean the fishers crouching in their boats, the farmers sweating through their grazing land, the barb in the mouth, the shot in the head, the chains of middlemen less tolerable than farmers or fishers, the organizations that prepare or can or pack, the transport firms, the financiers – Mihaly, you're laughing at me!"

"Ah, you're talking of all this organization with such disapproval. I approve. *Vive l'organisation!* And let me remind you that the new synthetic food plants are triumphs of organization. Last century, as you say, they didn't approve of prisons, but they had them, nevertheless; this century we have become organized, and we don't have prisons. Last century, indeed, they didn't approve of war, yet they had three bouncing big ones, in 1914, in 1939, and in 1969; this century we have become organized, and we hold our wars on Charon, the farthest planet, out of harm's way. If that's not civilization, I accept it readily as a substitute."

"So we all do. But it may only be a substitute, man's substitute. Notice that whatever we do, it is at someone else's or something else's expense."

"I gratefully accept their sacrifice. How will you have your steak, Hilary?"

"Oh, overdone, please. I can't quite bear the thought of it being real blood and animal tissue. All I'm trying to say is that our civilization may be built not on our best, but on our worst: on fear – other people's if not our own – or on greed. Can I pour you some more wine? And perhaps another species may have another idea of civilization, built on a sympathy for, an empathy with, all other living things. Perhaps these aliens —"

He pressed the spin stud in the oven pedestal. The porcelain and glass hemisphere slid into the bronze hemisphere. He retrieved the steaks. The aliens again! Ah, but Mrs. Warhoon was off form tonight! The platemaker coughed out two warm plates, and he served her moodily, without taking in what she was saying. Enlightened self-interest, he thought; that was the most you could or should expect from anyone; once you met an altruist, you had to beware a sick man or a scoundrel. Perhaps people like Mrs. Warhoon, who wouldn't face the fact, were sick too, and ought to be encouraged to enter mental therapy homes, like criminals and hot gospellers. Once you started questioning fundamentals, like a man's right to eat good red meat if he could afford it, then you were in trouble, even if you cared to think of that trouble as enlightenment.

"By the standards of another species," Mrs. Warhoon was saying, "our culture might merely seem like a sickness. It may be that sickness which prevents us from seeing how we ought to communicate with the aliens, rather than any shortcoming of theirs."

"It's an interesting theory, Hilary. You may have a chance to turn it into practice on a large scale shortly."

"Oh, indeed? You don't mean that some other ship has found more aliens at large in the universe, do you?"

"Nothing quite so fortunate as that. I received a long letter from Lattimore yesterday morning, which was partly why I invited you here this evening. The Americans, as you know, are very interested in our ETA's. We have had a constant stream of them to the Exozoo over the last month. They are convinced, and I am sure Lattimore has convinced them, that things are not being run as efficiently as they might be. Lattimore wrote to say that their new stellar exploration ship, *Gansas*, has been re-routed, though the re-routing is not official yet. Its investigation of the Crab Nebula is postponed. Instead, it will be heading for Clementina, to search for the home planet of the ETA's."

Mrs. Warhoon put her knife and fork together, raised her eyebrows, and said, "What?"

"Lattimore will be on the flight in an advisory capacity. His meeting with you much impressed him and he earnestly hopes that you will come along on the flight as chief cosmoclectic. He asked me to put in a good word for him before he gets in touch with you direct."

Mrs. Warhoon let her shoulders sag and leaned forward between the Scandinavian candelabras. "Goodness," she said. Her cheeks became red; in the candlelight she looked thirty again.

"He says you will not be the only woman on the flight. He also gives a rough indication of the salary, which will be fabulous. You ought to go, Hilary. It's a splendid opportunity."

She put an elbow on the table and rested her forehead on her hand. He thought it a theatrical gesture, even while seeing that she was genuinely moved and excited. His earlier fantasies returned to him.

"Space! You know I've been no farther abroad than Venus. You know it would wreck my marriage, Mihaly. Alfred would never forgive me."

"I'm sorry. I understood your marriage was a marriage in name only."

Her eyes rested blankly on a framed infra red photograph of Conquest Canyon, Pluto. She drained her wineglass.

"It doesn't matter. I can't – or possibly will not – save it. To leave in the *Gansas* would make a clean break with the past. . . . Thank goodness that in that sphere at least we are more civilized than our grandparents, and have no involved divorce laws. Should I go on the *Gansas*, Mihaly? I should, shouldn't I? You know there are few men I would as readily take advice from as you."

The curve of her wrist, the uncertain glimmer of candlelight in her hair, had helped him to make up his mind. He rose, went round the table, and placed his hands on her bare shoulders.

"You owe it to yourself, Hilary. You know it is not only a golden professional opportunity; these days, we are not adult humans until we have faced ourselves in deep space."

"Nuh ah, Mihaly, I know your reputation, and on the techni you promised you would take me to the new play.

81

Oughtn't we to be on our way?" She turned in her chair, away from him, so that he was forced to retreat. With as good a grace as he could muster, he suggested that they might walk, as the theatre was only just round the corner and it was impossible, in this war year, to catch taxis after dark.

"I'll go and put a new face on and prepare myself for the street," she said, retreating into the little toileteer that most expensive flats boasted these days. Secure behind the locked door, she surveyed her face in a mirror. She saw, not without satisfaction, that a slight flush spread over her cheeks. It was not the first time that Mihaly had tried something of this sort; she was not going to yield while it was well known that he had an Oriental mistress; because she was away on holiday at present was no reason to accept the post of substitute.

Men led enviable lives. They could pursue whims more easily than women. But here she had a chance to pursue something stronger than a whim: the desire to see distant planets. That that fascinating man Lattimore, Bryant Lattimore, would be on the *Gansas* too was an incidental, but one that made the prospect more exciting.

Daintily, she raised first her left arm, then her right, and sniffed. Okay there, but she gave it a burst of deodorant for luck.

Those little armpit glands were the only ones in the human body designed to produce smell, although a number of other glands and juices and secretions emitted it incidentally. The Japanese and some of the Chinese did not have that special gland; or if they did it was considered a pathological condition. Strange; she must ask Mihaly about it – he should know; his mistress was reputed to be Japanese or Chinese.

As she let her thoughts ramble and applied powder, she watched the flush fade from her cheeks. Perhaps it had been caused not by emotion but by the meat-of-animal she had consumed. She inspected the little white teeth arranged behind her red lips, liking the savagery of her smile.

"Grr, you little carnivore!" she whispered. She treated herself to a suspicion of perfume, an exclusive perfume that contained ambergris which (she hastily censored the image) is the undigested remnant of squid and octopus found in the intestines of the spermaceti whale. She touched up her hair, clipped on her street mask, and whisked superbly out to greet Pasztor.

He had already clipped his mask on. Together, they went down into the street.

War had not improved the city. Whereas other cities in other nations had long ago banished – or at least brought in legislation to deal with – various metropolitan abuses, London suffered under a multiplication of them.

Ash and rubbish bins stood all along the pavement, while the gutters were full of litter. The shortage of unskilled labour was crippling the city. This shortage had caused some streets to be closed to traffic, for their surfaces had become impassable, and there was nobody to repair them. Many people saw little to regret in this, for to pedestrians any relief from the heaving hooting traffic was welcome. As Mihaly walked along with Mrs. Warhoon, he sardonically said thanks for such gifts to civilization as their street masks, which alone guaranteed that they did not fall swooning from the waste gases pouring out of the cars snorting at their elbows.

Gigantic hoardings, covering a site where an office block had burnt down before a fire engine could crawl four blocks to save it, announced that Holidays At Home were Fun, as well as being in the national interest; that Death could be turned to Financial Account by bequeathing one's body to Burgess's Body Chemicals; and that Gonorrhoea was Out of Control, with a graph to prove it, by courtesy of the World Gonorrhoea Year. There was also a smaller poster issued by MINIGAG, the Ministry of

Gastronomy and Agriculture, proclaiming that animal foods caused premature ageing and that man-made foods contained no toxics; the point was rammed deftly home by two pictures, one of an old man having a heart attack, one of a young girl having a synthash.

Mercifully, most of this townscape was wrapped in a decent obscurity, since power cuts imposed semi-blackouts on the capital's gaiety every night.

"Walking here, I can hardly think of walking on a different planet," Mrs. Warhoon said.

"You certainly don't get much sight of the universe here," Pasztor said, speaking above the snarl of engines.

"In another two or three centuries, mankind will have a different outlook on life and the rules by which he lives. He will have digested the universe into his art, architecture, customs, everything. As yet we're adolescents. The city's our savage playground." She gestured at a shop window exhibiting one enormous motor bike, shaped like a system-ship and glittering like El Dorado. "It's a place where we undergo perpetual initiation rites, ordeals by fire, crowds, and gas. We aren't mature enough to deal with your ETA's."

With a shock, Mihaly thought, "My God, she's tight! We drank real wine and she's probably used to synth-wine. . . ." She went on talking, even when he clutched her arm so that she would not trip over the old newspapers blowing about their feet.

"We started wrongly with those creatures, Mihaly, by making them adhere to our rules instead of studying theirs. Perhaps the *Gansas* will find more of them and we will have another chance to make contact, on their terms."

"As yet we don't know what their terms are. Should we respect their inclination to live in their own waste products? We could let them accumulate this – er, matter, as they seem disposed to do. You know I suggested that. But it is – well, it's malodorous, and poor old Bodley and his

84

staff have to work in there with them. . . ."

He was glad to get her to the theatre.

The play was a jolly send-up of the Cold War era, a non-musical version of *West Side Story*, played in quaint pre-World War III costume. Both Pasztor and Mrs. Warhoon enjoyed it; but her mind kept drifting back to the prospect of making vacuum with the *Gansas*, so that in the interval Pasztor threw himself into the free-for-all struggle round the theatre bar rather than let her start another discussion. As they came out of the theatre at the end of the play, she insisted she must go home, and he competed with evening dresses and uniforms to cram into one of the sinkers that rose to connect with the district shuttle. It had rained during their incarceration, clearing the city air somewhat. Drops of oily water splashed on them from the overhead rail; still Mrs. Warhoon stuck bravely to her subject.

"Do you remember Wittgenbacher's saying that our intelligence might merely be an instinct for space?"

"I have thought about it," he said, elbowing forward.

"Do you think I'll be following my instinct if I join the *Gansas*?"

He looked at her, tall and still fairly slender, her eyes attractive over her mask.

"What's wrong with you this evening, Hilary? What do you want me to say to you?"

"You could tell me for instance whether I am going into deep space to integrate myself – to become matured away from my womb world and all that sort of thing – or whether I am doing it to flee from an unsatisfactory marriage I would be better employed mending."

A man in astrogator's uniform wedged behind her looked at her in sudden interest as he caught part of this remark.

"I don't know you well enough to answer that," Mihaly said.

"Nobody does." She spoke the words dismissively, smiling, for he had finally got her to the doors of the sinker. She touched his fingers and passed in. Pasztor had to fight not to be carried in as well.

The doors closed, the pellet was sucked up its tube. He watched its lights rise up to the level of the monobus rail. A globule of water splashed into his left eye. He turned and made his way home through emptying streets.

Back in his flat over the Exozoo, he walked about aimlessly, thinking. Clearing the remains of their meal away, he swept cutlery and dishes from the dining-table into the disposer, watching soft flame rise as they disintegrated. Then he resumed his pacing.

Hilary had a grain of truth among her chaff, though earlier in the evening he had mentally labelled it sickness. Wasn't truth a sickness man spent a lifetime seeking, just as a dog seeks the coarse grass that makes it vomit? What was that epigram that he had trotted forth too often, about civilization being the distance man placed between himself and his excreta? But it was nearer the truth to say that civilization was the distance man had placed between himself and everything else, for cradled deep in the concept of culture was the need for privacy. Once away from the hurly-burly of camp fires, man invented rooms, barriers, behind which he developed his most characteristic practices. Meditation arose from mere abstraction, the individual arts arose from folk crafts, love arose from sex, the concept of the individual arose from the tribe.

But were the barriers valuable when one faced another culture? And again, mightn't one of the difficulties with coming to grips with ETA's be that you hardly realized how strong a hold the mores of your own culture had on you?

It was, Pasztor thought, what might be called a Good Question, and damn it, he would act on it now.

He took the lift down to the ground floor. The Exozoo

86

was dark about him; only the simultaneously shrill and deep chuckle of a stone-cracker in the High-G House sent a shiver through the darkness. Man, shut in his culture, so anxious to imprison other animals with him. . . .

The two ETA's were seemingly asleep as he entered and the pallid lights came on. One of the lizard creatures took a flying leap back into the arm socket of its protector, but the big bulk did not stir.

Pasztor moved through the side door and so came into the back of the cage. He unlocked the low barrier and walked up to the ETA's. They opened their eyes with what looked like infinite weariness.

"Don't worry, fellows. I'm sorry to trouble you, but a certain lady who has your interests at heart has given me, all unwittingly, a new line of approach. Look, fellows, I'm trying to be friendly, see. I do want to reach across, if it can be done."

Removing his trousers, squatting close to them, speaking gently, the director of the Exozoo defecated on to the plastic floor.

CHAPTER EIGHT

"How far-seeing you were to christen this world Grudgrodd, Cosmopolitan," the third Politan said.

"I've explained several times my reason for thinking that we cannot any longer be on Grudgrodd," said the

Sacred Cosmopolitan, as the two utods lay comfortably together.

"And I still say that I don't believe metal could be made strong enough to withstand launching into the star-realms. Don't forget I took a course in metal-fracture when I was a priestling. Besides, the metal thing wasn't the right shape for a spaceship. I know it doesn't do to be too dogmatic, but there are some points on which one has to make a stand: though I do it with regards to your cosmopolity only with apologies."

"Say what you may, I have the feeling in my bones that the Triple suns no longer shine on these skies – not that these thin lifeforms ever permit us to see the skies."

As he spoke, the Sacred Cosmopolitan swivelled one of his heads to watch the thin lifeform performing his natural function a few feet distant. He thought he recognized this thin lifeform as one of those whose habits did not arouse disgust; certainly he was not the one who came with an attachment that spurted a jet of cold water. Nor did he seem to be one of those who sat about with machines and two assistants (no doubt they were this world's equivalents of the priesthood) so palpably trying to seduce him and the third Politan into communication.

The thin lineform stood up and assembled the cloth over the lower part of his body.

"That is very interesting!" the Politan exclaimed. "It confirms what we were saying a couple of days ago."

"In most particulars, yes. As we thought, they have two heads as we do, but one is for dunging and one for speaking."

"What seems so laughable is that they have a pair of legs sticking out of their lower heads. Yes, perhaps after all you are right, father-mother; despite all logic, perhaps we really are spirited far away from the Triple Suns, for it is difficult to imagine any of this sort of horrid absurdity on the planets under their sway. Why do you think he came to perform a dung ritual here?"

The Cosmopolitan twiddled one of his fingers in a motion of bafflement.

"He can hardly regard this as a sacred seeding spot. It may be that he performed merely to let us see that we were not the only ones possessing fertility; or on the other hand, it may have been merely from curiosity, in order to see what we did. Here's a case again, I think, where for the time being we must admit that the thinlegs' ways of thought are too alien for us to interpret, and that any tentative explanation we may offer is bound to be utodomorphic. And while we're on the subject. . . . I don't want to alarm you in any way . . . no, as Cosmopolitan, I must keep these things to myself."

"Please – since there have been only the two of us, you have told me many things from the rich store of your mind that you would not otherwise have told me. Snort on, I beg you."

The alien lifeform was standing near by, watching. He was unable to maintain stillness for any length of time. Ignoring him, the Cosmopolitan began to speak cautiously, for he knew on what dangerous ground he trod. When one of his grorgs began to crawl under his belly, he slapped it back into position with a firmness that surprised even himself.

"I don't want you to be alarmed at what I am about to say, son, though I am aware that I may seem at first to strike at the very foundations of our belief. You remember that moment when the thinlegs came to us in the dark, when we were in the midden by the side of the star-realmark?"

"Though it seems a long while ago, I do not forget it."

"The thinlegs came to us then and immediately translated the others into their carrion stage."

"I remember. I was startled at first. I crept close to you."

89

"And then?"

"When they were taking us in their wheeled truck, to the tall metal thing you say may have been a star-realm-ark, I was so overcome with shame that I had not been chosen to move further along the utodammp cycle, that I hardly took in any other impressions."

The thinlegs was making signals with the mouth of his upper head, but they moved on to a higher audibility band, as was appropriate when discussing personal aspects, and ignored him from then on.

The Sacred Cosmopolitan continued, "My son, I find this difficult to say, since our language naturally does not hold the appropriate concepts, but these lifeforms may be as alien in thought as they are in shape: not just in their upper thoughts, but in their whole psychological constitution. For a long while I felt as you did, a sort of shame that our six companions had been chosen for translation while we hadn't. But ... supposing, Blug Lugug, that these lifeforms did not exercise choice, suppose they translated us at random."

"Random? I'm surprised to hear you use such a vulgar word, Cosmopolitan. The fall of a leaf or the splash of a raindrop may be – er, random, but with higher lifeforms – everything higher than a mud snwitch – the fact that they form part of life cycles prevents anything random."

"That applies to beings on the worlds of the Triple Suns. But these creatures of Grudgrodd, these thinlegs, may be part of another and conflicting pattern."

At this point, the lifeform left them. As he disappeared, the light faded from their room. Quite uninterested in these minor phenomena, the Cosmopolitan continued to grope for words.

"What I am saying is that in some ways these creatures may not have helpful intentions for us. There is a word from the Revolution Age that is useful here; these thinlegs may be *bad*. Do you know this word from your studies?"

"It's a sort of sickness, isn't it?" the Politan asked, recalling the years when he had wallowed through the mazes of mindsuckle in the epoch of Welcome White.

"Well, a special sort of sickness. I feel that these thin-legs are bad in a more healthy way."

"Is that why you have not wished us to communicate with them?"

"Certainly not. I am no more prepared to converse with strangers bereft of my wallow than they would probably be prepared to converse with me bereft of the body materials that cover them. In the end, when they grasp that rudimentary fact, we may perhaps try to talk to them, though I suspect their brains may be quite as limited as their voice range suggests. But we shall certainly get nowhere until they realize we have certain basic requirements; once they have grasped that, talk may be worth while."

"This ... this business of *bad*. I'm alarmed you should think like this."

"Son, the more I consider what has happened, the more I am forced to do so."

Blug Lugug, who had been known for a hundred and eighty years as a third Politan, lapsed into a troubled silence.

He was recalling more and more about *bad*.

In the Revolution Age, there had been bad. Even though the utods lived up to eleven hundred years, the Revolution Age was over three thousand generations ago; yet its effects still lingered in everyday life on Dapdrof.

At the beginning of that amazing age was born Manna Warun. It was significant that he had been hatched during a particularly cataclysmic entropic solar orbital disestablishment, the very esod, in fact, during which Dapdrof, changing from Saffron Smiler to Yellow Scowler, had lost its little moon, Woback, which now pursued its own eccentric course alone.

91

Manna Warun had collected disciples and left the traditional wallows and salads of his people. His band had moved to the wastes, there to spend many years refining and developing the ancient and traditional skills of the utods. Some of his group left him; more joined. There they stayed for one hundred and seventy-five years, according to the old priestly histories.

During that time, they created what Manna Warun called "an industrial revolution". They learnt to make many more metals than their contemporaries knew of: hard metals, metals that could stretch thin and convey new forms of power along their lengths. The revolutionaries scorned to walk on their own six feet any more. Now they rode in various sorts of car that boasted a multitude of tumbling feet, or they flew in the air in other cars with wings. So said the old legends, though there was no doubt that they liked to lay it on a bit thick.

But when the revolutionaries came back to their people to try and convert them to new doctrines, one feature of their lives in particular seemed strange. For the revolutionaries preached – and dramatically practised – what they called "cleanliness".

The mass of the people (if the old reports were to be believed) were well disposed towards most of the proposed innovations. They were particularly pleased with the notion that terms of motherhood might be eased by introducing one or more systems that would abolish mindsuckle; because for most of the fifty years of a utod's childhood a mother was committed to mindsuckling her child on the complicated law and lore that was racial history and habit; and the revolutionaries taught that this function might be handled by mechanism. But "cleanliness" was something different altogether – a real revolution.

Cleanliness was a difficult thing to grasp, if only because it attacked the very roots of being. It suggested that the warm mud banks in which the utod had evolved might now be abandoned, that the wallows and middensteads and middens which were effective mud-substitutes be abandoned, that the little parasite-devouring grorgs which were the traditional utodian companions be also abandoned.

Manna and his disciples demonstrated that it was possible to live without all this needless luxury ("dirt" was another term they used for it). The cleanliness was evidence of progress. That in the modern revolutionary age, mud was *bad*.

In this way, the revolutionaries had turned necessity into virtue. Working in the wastes, far away from the wallows and their sheltering ammps, mud and liquid had been scarce. In that austerity had been born their austere creed.

They went further. Once he had started, Manna Warun developed his theme, and attacked the established beliefs of the utods. In this he was aided by his chief disciple, Creezeazs. Creezeazs denied that the spirits of utods were born into their infant bodies from the ammps; he denied that a carrion stage followed the corporeal stage. Or rather, he could not gainsay that the bodily elements of the corporeal stage were absorbed into the mud and so drawn up again into the ammps, but he claimed that there was no similar transference for a spirit. He had no proof of this. It was just an emotional statement obviously aimed at getting the utod away from their natural habit; yet he found those who believed him.

Strange moral laws, prohibitions, inhibitions, began to grow up among the believers. But it could not be denied that they had power. The cities of the wastes to which they withdrew blazed with light in the dark. They cultivated the lands by strange methods, and drew strange fruit from them. They took to covering their casspu orifices. They changed from male to female at unprecedented rates, indulging themselves without breeding. All this and more they did. Yet it was not noticeable that they were exactly happier – not that they preached happiness, for their talk was more of duty and rights and of what was considered good or bad.

One great thing that the revolutionaries achieved in their cities stirred everyone's imagination.

The utods had many poetic qualities, as their vast fund of tales, epics, songs, chants, and werewhispers show. This side of them was touched when the revolutionaries built some of their machinery into an ancient ammp seed and drove it into and far beyond the skies. Manna Warun went in it.

Since pre-memory days, before mindsuckle had made the races of utod what they were, the ammp seeds had been used for boats with which to sail to less crowded parts of Dapdrof. To sail to less crowded worlds had a sort of crazy appropriateness in it. Down in the wallows, the complicated nexi of old families began to feel that perhaps after all cleanliness had something. The fifteen worlds that circled about the six planets of the Home Cluster were all visible at various times to the naked eye, and hence were known and admired. To experience the thrill of visiting them might even be worth renouncing "dirt".

People, converts and perverts, began to trickle into the cities of the wastes.

Then something odd happened.

The word began to get about that Manna Warun was not all he had made himself out to be. It was said that he had often slid away to indulge himself in a secret wallow, for instance. Rumours spread thick and fast, and of course Manna was not there to deny them.

As the ugly rumours grew, people wondered when Creezeazs would step forward and clear his leader's name.

At last, Creezeazs did step forward. Heavily, with tears in his eyes, speaking through his ockpu orifices only, he

94

admitted that the stories circulating were true. Manna was a sinner, a tyrant, a mud-bather. He had none of the virtues he demanded from others. In fact, though others – his friend and true disciple Creezeazs in particular – had done all in their power to stop him, Manna had gone to the *bad*. Now that the sad tale had emerged, there was nothing for it. Manna Warun must go. It was in the public interest. Nobody, of course, would be happy about it; but there was such a thing as duty. People had a right to be protected, otherwise the good would be destroyed with the bad.

Hardly a utod liked all this, although they saw Creezeazs' point of view; Manna must be expelled. When the prophet returned from the stars, there was a reception committee waiting for him on the star-realm-ark field.

Before the ark landed, trouble broke out. A young utod, whose shining but alarmingly cracked skin showed him to be a thorough-going Hygienic (as the Corps of the Revolution were currently calling themselves), jumped up on to a box. He deretracted all his limbs and cried in a voice like a steam whistle that Creezeazs had been lying about Manna to serve his own ends. All who followed Creezeazs were traitors.

At this moment, an unprecedented event occurred, occurred even as the star-realm-ark floated down from the skies: fighting broke out, and a utod with a sharp metal rod hastened Creezeazs on to the next stage of his utod-ammp cycle.

"Creezeazs!" gasped the third Politan.

"What make you mention that unfortunate name?" inquired the Cosmopolitan.

"I was thinking about the Revolution Age. Creezeazs is the first utod in our history to be propelled along the utod-ammp cycle without goodwill," Blug Lugug said, coming back to the present.

"That was a bad time. But perhaps because these thinlegs also seem to enjoy cleanliness, they also hasten people round the cycle without goodwill. As I say, they are bad in a healthy way. And we are their random victims."

Blug Lugug withdrew his limbs as much as possible. He shut his eyes, closed his orifices, and stretched himself until his external appearance was that of an enormous terrestrial sausage. This was his way of expressing priestly alarm.

There was nothing in their situation to warrant the cosmopolitan's extreme language. True, it might become rather dull if they were kept here for any length of time – one needed a change of scenery every five years or so. And it was thoughtless the way the lifeforms removed the signs of their fertility. But the lifeforms showed evidence of goodwill: they supplied food, and soon learned not to bring items that were unwelcome. With time and patience, they might learn other useful things.

On the other hand, there was this question of *bad*. It was indeed possible that the lifeforms had the same sort of madness that existed in the Revolution Age of Dapdrof. Yet it was absurd to pretend that, however alien they might be, these thinlegs did not have an equivalent evolutionary cycle to the utodammp cycle; and this, being so fundamental, could only be something for which they would have a profound respect – in their own peculiar way, naturally.

And there was this: the Revolution Age was a freak, a mere flash in the pan, lasting only for five hundred years – half a lifespan – out of the hundreds of millions of years of utodammp memory. It would seem rather a tall coincidence if the thinlegs happened to be undergoing the same trouble at this moment.

It was notorious that people who used violent words like *bad* and *random victim*, the very words of madness, were themselves verging on madness. So the Sacred Cosmopolitan. . . .

At the very thought, the Politan quivered. His fondness for the Cosmopolitan was deepened by the fact that the older utod, during one of his female phases, had mothered him. Now he stood in need of consolation by the other members of his wallow; clearly, it was time they were getting back to Dapdrof.

That implied that they should speak with these aliens and hasten their return. The Cosmopolitan forbad communication – and quite rightly – on a point of etiquette; but it began to look more and more as if something should be done. Perhaps, Blug Lugug thought, he could get one of the aliens on his own and try to convey some sense to it. It shouldn't be difficult; he had memorized every sentence they had spoken in his presence since their arrival in the metal thing; although it made no sense to him, it should be useful somehow.

Pursing one of his ockpu orifices, he said, "Wilfred, you don't happen to have a screwdriver in your pocket, do you?"

"What's that?" asked the Cosmopolitan.

"Nothing. Thinlegs-talk."

Sinking into a silence that held less cheer than usual, the third Politan began to think about the Revolution Age, in case it had any useful parallels with the present case to offer.

With the death of Creezeazs and the return home of Manna Warun, more trouble had begun. This was when *bad* had flourished at its grandest. Quite a number of utods were thrust without goodwill into the next phase of their cycle. Manna, of course, returned from his flight in the star-realm-ark very vexed to find how things had turned against him in the Cities of the Wastes.

He became more extreme than before. His people were to forswear mud-bathing entirely; instead, water would be supplied to every dwelling. They were to keep their casspu orifices covered. Skin oils were forbidden. Greater industry

97

was required. And so on.

But the seeds of dissatisfaction had been well sown by Creezeazs and his followers, and more blood-shedding ensued. Many people returned to their ancestral wallows, leaving the Cities of the Wastes slowly to fall into ruin while the inhabitants fought each other. Everyone regretted this, since there existed a genuine admiration for Manna which nothing could quench.

In particular, his journey among the stars was widely discussed and praised. Much was known, even at that period, about the neighbouring celestial bodies known as the Home Cluster, and particularly about the three suns, Welcome White, Saffron Smiler, and Yellow Scowler, around each of which Dapdrof revolved in turn as one esod followed another. These suns, and the other planets in the cluster, were as familiar – and as strange – to the people as the Circumpolar Mountains in Dapdrof's Northern Shunkshukkun.

Whatever woes the Revolution Age had brought, it had brought the chance to investigate these other places. It was a chance the ordinary utod found he wanted.

The Hygienics had control of all star-realm travel. The masses of the unconverted, pilgrimaging from all over the globe to the Cities of the Wastes, found they could partake in the new exploration of other worlds under one of two conditions. They could become converts to the harsh disciplines of Manna Warun, or they could mine the materials needed for building and fuelling the engines of the arks. Most of them preferred to do the latter.

Mining came easily; had not the utod evolved from little burrowing creatures not unlike the Haprafruf Mud Mole? They dug the ores willingly, and soon the whole process of building star arks became routine, almost as much a folk art as weaving, platting, or blishing. So in turn travel through the star realms took on something of the same informality, particularly when it was discovered that the

Triple Suns and their three near neighbours supported seven other worlds on which life could be lived almost as enjoyably as on Dapdrof.

Then came a time when life indeed was rather pleasant on some of the other worlds: on Buskey, for instance, and Clabshub, where the utodammp system was quickly established. Meanwhile the Hygienics split into rival sects, those that practised retraction of all limbs, and those that deplored it as immoral. Finally, the three nuclear Wars of Wise Deportment broke out, and the fair face of the home planet underwent a thoroughly unhygienic bombardment, the severity of which – destroying as it did so many miles of carefully tended forest and swamp land – actually changed climatic conditions for a period of about a century.

The resulting upheavals in the weather, followed by a chain of severe winters, concluded the wars in the most radical of ways, by converting into the carrion stage almost all the surviving Hygienics of whatever persuasion. Manna himself disappeared; his end was never known for sure, although legend had it that a particularly fine ammp, growing in the midst of the ruins of the largest of the Cities of the Wastes, represented the next stage of his existence.

Slowly, the old and more reasonable ways returned.

Helped by utods returning from the other planets, the home population re-established itself. Dams were rebuilt, swamps painstakingly restored, middensteads reintroduced on the traditional patterns, ammps re-planted everywhere. The Cities of the Wastes were left to fall into decay. Nobody was interested any more in the ethics of cleanliness. Law and ordure were restored.

Yet at whatever expense it had been acquired, the industrial revolution had borne its fruits, and not all of them were permitted to die. The basic techniques necessary for maintaining star-realm travel passed to the ancient priesthood dedicated to maintaining the happiness of the people. The priesthood simplified practices already smoothed into quasi-ritual by habit and saw that these techniques were handed on from mother to son by mindsuckle, together with the rest of the racial lore.

All that now lay three thousand generations and almost as many esods ago. Through the disciplines of mindsuckle, its outlines remained clear. In Blug Lugug's brains, the memory of the hideous perverted talk and teachings of Manna and other Hygienics was vivid. He prided himself on being the filthiest and healthiest of his generation of priests. And he knew by the absurd phrases of moral condemnation the Cosmopolitan had uttered that the cleanliness inflicted on his old body by the thinlegs was affecting his brains. It was time something was done.

CHAPTER NINE

It was an American sage back in the nineteenth century who coined the slogan since used so successfully on the wrappers of every Happy Hypersleep tablet, "The mass of men live lives of quiet desperation." Thoreau certainly had a point when he observed that anxiety and even misery feed in the breast of those often most concerned with putting up a brave show of happiness; yet such is the constitution of human nature that the reverse holds equally true, and under conditions commonly regarded as most likely to create misery, a man may lead a life of quiet happiness.

The gates of St. Alban's prison swung open and emitted the prison bus. It bowled out beneath the aluminium legend over the portal that read "To Understand Is To Forgive", and headed for the region of the metropolis called The Gay Ghetto.

Or so the area was most generally known. Its inhabitants called it The Knackers, or Joburg, or Wonderland, or Sucker City, or indeed any less savoury name that occurred to them. The area had been established by a government enlightened enough to realize that some men, while being far from criminal in intent, are incapable of living within the exacting framework of civilization; which is to say that they do not share the goals and incentives of the majority of their fellow beings; which is to say that they see no point in working from ten till four day in and day out for the privilege of maintaining a woman in wedlock and x or n number of children. This body of men, which numbered geniuses and neurotics in equal proportions (frequently within the same anatomy), was allowed to settle within the Gay Ghetto, which – because it was unsupervised in any way by the forces of law – soon became the nesting ground also of criminals. Within the ruinous square mile of this human game reserve, a unique society formed; it looked at the monstrous machinery of living that ground on beyond its walls with the same mixture of fear and moral disapproval with which the monstrous machinery regarded it.

The prison taxi halted at the end of a steep brick street. The two released prisoners, Rodney Walthamstone and his ex-cell mate, climbed out. At once the taxi swerved and drove away, its door automatically sliding shut as it went.

Walthamstone looked about him with unease.

The drearily respectable dolls' houses on either side of

101

the street hunched their thin shoulders behind dog-soiled railings, averting their gaze from the strip of waste that began where they left off.

Beyond the waste rose the wall of the Gay Ghetto. Some of the wall was wall; some of it was formed from little old houses into which concrete had been poured until the little old houses were solid.

"Is this it?" Walthamstone asked.

"This is it, Wal. This is freedom. We can live here without anybody mucking us about."

The early sunshine, a snaggle-toothed old trickster, lay its transient gold and broken shadows across the uninviting flank of the Ghetto, of Joburg, of Paradise, of Bums' Berg, of Queer Street, of Floppers. Tid started towards it, saw that Walthamstone hesitated, grasped his hand, and pulled him along.

"I ought to write to my old Aunt Flo and Hank Quilter and tell 'em what I'm doing," Walthamstone said. He stood between the old life and the new, naturally fearful. Although Tid was his own age, Tid was so much more sure of himself.

"You can think about that later," Tid said.

"There was other blokes on the starship. . . ."

"Like I tell you, Wal, only suckers allow themselves to enlist on spaceships. I got a cousin Jack, he signed on for Charon; he's perched out on that miserable billiard ball, fighting Brazilians. Come *on*, Wal."

The grubby hand tightened on the grubby wrist.

"Perhaps I'm being stupid. Perhaps I got all mixed up in jug," Walthamstone said.

"That's what jug is meant for."

"My poor old aunt. She's always been so kind to me."

"Don't make me weep. You know I'll be kind to you too."

Giving up the gruelling battle to express himself, Walthamstone moved forward and was led like a lost soul towards the entrance to Avernus. But the ascent to this Avernus was not easy. No portals stood wide. They climbed over rubble and litter towards the solid houses.

One of the houses had a door which creaked open when Tid pulled it. A tongue of sunlight licked in with their untrusting glances. Within, the solid concrete had been chipped into a sort of chimney with steps in the side. Without another word to his friend, Tid began to climb; left with no option, Walthamstone followed. In the gloom on either side of him he saw tiny grottoes, some no bigger than open mouths; and there were cysts and bubbles; and clots and blemishes; all of which had formed in the liquid concrete when it had first been poured down through the rafters and engulfed the house.

The chimney brought them out to an upper window at the back. Tid gave a cheer and turned to help Walthamstone.

They squatted on the window-sill. The ground sloped down from the sill, where it had been piled as an embankment for no other apparent purpose than to grow as fine a crop of cow parsley, tall grass, and elder as you could wish to see.

This wilderness was divided by paths, some of which ran round the upper windows of the solid houses, some of which sloped down into the Ghetto. Already people stirred there, a child of seven ran naked, whooping from doorstep to doorstep with a newspaper hat on its head. Ancient façades grew down into the earth, tatty and grand with a patina of old dirt and new sun.

"Me dear old shanty town!" Tid cried. He ran down one of the tracks, a foam of flower about his knees.

Hesitating only a moment, Walthamstone ran down after his lover.

Bruce Ainson assumed his coat with a fine air of desperation, while Enid stood at the other end of the hall, watching him with her hands clasped. He wanted her to

103

start to speak, so that he could say, "Don't say anything!", but she had nothing else to say. He looked sideways at her, and a shaft of compassion pierced through his self-concern.

"Don't worry," he said.

She smiled, made a gesture. He closed the door and was gone.

Outside, he paid ten tubbies into the corner sinker and rose to the local traffic level. Abstractedly, he climbed into a moving chair that skied him up to the non-stop level and racked itself on to one of the robot monobuses. As he sped towards distant London, Bruce dwelt on the scene he had just made with Enid after the news in the paper hit him.

Yes, he had behaved badly. He had behaved badly because he did not, in such a crisis, see the point of behaving well. One was as moral as one could be, as well-intentioned, as well-controlled, as intelligent, as *innocent*; and then the flood of days brought down with it (from some ghastly unseen headwaters, whence it had been travelling for unguessed time) some vile foetid thing that had to be faced and survived. Why should one behave other than badly before such beastliness?

Now the mood, the shaky exhilaration of the mood, was passing. He had shed it on Enid. He would have to behave well before Mihaly.

But did life have to be quite so vile a draught? Dimly, he recognized one of the drives that had carried him through the years of study necessary to gain him his Master Explorer's certificate. He had hoped to find a world, hiding beyond reach of sight of Earth in the dark light years, a world of beings for whom diurnal existence was not such an encumbrance to the spirit. He wanted to know how it was done.

Now it looked as if he'd never have the chance again.

Reaching the tremendous new Outflank Ring that

104

circled high about outer London, Ainson changed on to a district level and headed for the quarter where Sir Mihaly Pasztor worked. Ten minutes later, he was stalling impatiently before the Director's secretary.

"I doubt if he can see you this morning, Mr. Ainson, since you have no appointment."

"He has to see me, my dear girl; will you please announce me?"

Pecking doubtfully at the nail of her little finger, the girl disappeared into the inner office. She emerged a minute later, standing aside without speaking to admit Ainson into Mihaly's room. Ainson swept by her with irritation; that was a girl he had always been careful to smile and nod at; her answering show of friendliness had been nothing but pretence.

"I'm sorry to interrupt you when it's obvious you are very busy," he said to the Director. Mihaly did not immediately assure his old friend that it was perfectly all right. He maintained a steady pacing by the window and asked, "What brings you here, Bruce? How's Enid?"

Ignoring the irrelevance of this last question, Ainson said, "I should think you might guess what has brought me here."

"It would be better if you told me."

Pulling a newspaper from his pocket, Ainson dropped it on Pasztor's desk.

"You must have seen the paper. This confounded American ship, the *Gansas*, or whatever it's called, leaves next week to look for the home planet of our ETA's."

"I hope they will have luck."

"Don't you realize the absolute disgrace of it? I have not been invited to join the expedition. Every day I expected a word from them. It hasn't come. Surely there must be a mistake?"

"I think it is impossible there should be a mistake in such a matter, Bruce."

"I see. Then it's a public disgrace." Ainson stood there looking at his friend. Or was he really a friend? Was it not a gross misuse of the term, just because they had been acquainted for a number of years? He had admired the many sides of Pasztor's character, had admired him for the success of his technidramas, had admired his leadership on the First Charon Expedition, had admired him for being a man of action. Now he saw more deeply; he saw that this was merely a playboy of action, a dramatist's idea of a man of action, an imitation that revealed its spuriousness at last by the calmness with which, from his safe seat at the Exozoo, he watched his friend's discomfiture.

"Mihaly, although I am a year older than you, I am not yet ready to accept a safe seat back on Earth; I'm a man of action, and I'm still capable of action. I think I can say without false modesty that they still have need of men like me at the frontiers of the known universe. I was the man who discovered the ETA's, and I haven't forgotten that, if others have. I should be on the *Gansas* when she goes into TP next week. You could still pull strings and get me on to her, if you wanted. I ask you – I beg you to do this for me, and swear I will never ask you another favour. I just cannot bear the disgrace of being passed over in a vital moment like this."

Mihaly pulled a wry face, cupped an elbow and rubbed his chin.

"Would you care for a drink, Bruce?"

"Certainly not. Why do you always insist on offering me one when you know I don't drink?"

"You must excuse me if I have a little one. It is not normally my habit at this early time of morning." As he went over to a pair of small doors set in the wall, he said, "Perhaps you will feel better, or perhaps worse, if I tell you that you are not alone in your disgrace. Here at the Exozoo we have our disappointments. We have not made the progress in communication with these poor ETA's that we had hoped to do."

"I thought that one of them had suddenly started spouting English?"

"Spouting is right. A series of jumbled phrases with amazingly accurate imitations of the various voices that originally spoke them. I recognized my own voice quite clearly. Of course we have it all on tape. But, unfortunately, this development did not come soon enough to save the axe from falling. I have received word from the Minister for Extra-Terrestrial Affairs that all research with the ETA's is to close down forthwith."

Unwilling though he was to be diverted from his own concerns, Ainson was startled.

"By the Buzzardian universe! They *can't* just close it down! This – we've got here the most important thing that has ever happened in the history of man. They – I don't understand. They can't close it down."

Pasztor poured himself a small whisky and sipped it.

"Unfortunately, the Minister's attitude is understandable enough. I'm as shocked at this development as you are, Bruce, but I see how it comes about. It is not easy to make the general public or even a minister see that the business of understanding another race – or even deciding how its intelligence is to be measured beside ours – is not something that can be done in a couple of months. Let me put it bluntly, Bruce; you are thought to have been lax, and the suspicion has spread – just a feeling in the winds, no more – that we are similarly at fault. That feeling has made the minister's job a little more easy, that is all."

"But he cannot stop the work Bodley Temple and the others are doing."

"I went to see him last evening. He has stopped it. This afternoon the ETA's are being handed over to the Exobiology Department."

"Exobiology! Why, Mihaly, why? There is a conspiracy!"

107

"With an optimism I personally regard as unfounded, the Minister reasons like this. Within a couple of months, the *Gansas* will have located more ETA's – a whole planet full of them, in fact. Many of the basic questions, such as how far advanced the creatures are, will then be answered, and on the basis of those answers a new and much more effective attempt to communicate with them can be launched."

A sort of shaking took Ainson's body. This confirmed all he had ever suspected about the powers ranged against him. Blindly, he took a lighted mescahale from Pasztor and sucked its fragrance into his lungs. Slowly his vision cleared; he said, "Supposing all this were so; something more must lie behind the minister's move."

The Director helped himself to another drink.

"I inferred as much myself last evening. The minister gave me a reason which, like it or not, we must accept."

"What was the reason?"

"The war. We are comfortable here, we are apt to forget this crippling war with Brazil that has dragged on for so long. Brazil have captured Square 503, and it looks as if our casualties have been higher than announced. What interests the government at present more than the possibility of talking with the ETA's is the possibility that they do not experience pain. If there is some substance circulating in their arteries that confers complete analgesia, then the government want to know about it. It is obviously a potential war weapon.

"So, the official reasoning goes, we must find out how these beings tick. We must make the best use of them."

Ainson rubbed his head. The war! More insanity! It had never entered his mind.

"I knew it would happen! I knew it would! So they are going to cut our two ETA's up," he said. His voice sounded like a creaking door.

"They are going to cut them up in the most refined way.

They are going to sink electrodes into their brains, to see if pain can be induced. They will try a little over-heating here, a little freezing there. In short, they will try to discover if the ETA's freedom from pain really exists: and if it exists, whether it is engendered by a natural insensitivity or brought about by an anti-body. I have protested against the whole business, but I might as well have kept quiet. I'm as upset as you are."

Ainson clenched a fist and shook it vigorously close to his stomach.

"Lattimore is behind all this. I knew he was my enemy directly I saw him! You should never have let —"

"Oh don't be foolish, Bruce! Lattimore has nothing whatever to do with it. Can't you see this is the sort of bloody stupid thing that happens whenever something important is involved. It's the people who have the power rather than the people who have the knowledge who get the ultimate say. Sometimes I really think mankind is a bit mad."

"They're all mad. Fancy not begging me to go on the *Gansas*! I discovered these creatures, I know them! The *Gansas* needs me! You must do what you can, Mihaly, for the sake of an old friend."

Grimly, Pasztor shook his head.

"I can do nothing for you. I have explained why I myself am temporarily not very much in favour. You must do what you can for yourself, as we all must. Besides, there is a war on."

"Now you are using that same excuse! People have all been against me, always. My father was. So's my wife, my son – now you. I thought better of you, Mihaly. It's a public disgrace if I'm not on the *Gansas* when she hits vacuum, and I don't know what I'll do."

Mihaly shifted uncomfortably, hugged his whisky glass and stared at the floor.

"You didn't really expect better of me, Bruce. At heart,

you know you never expect better of anybody."

"I certainly shan't in future. You don't wonder a man grows bitter. My God, what really is there to live for!"

He stood up, stubbing the end of his mescahale into a disposer. "I can see myself out," he said.

In a state approaching elevation, he left the room, forging past the covertly interested secretary. Of course he didn't feel as badly as he led Mihaly, that trumped up little Hungarian, to believe; it would do the fellow good to see that some people had real sufferings, and weren't just poseurs.

He fell back on an earlier track of thought. You didn't go through the business of searching for new planets – with all the sweat and sacrifice that that entailed – merely because you hoped some day to find a race of beings to whom life was not just a burden for anyone with any sort of sensitivity. No, there was another side to that coin! You went because life on Earth was such hell, because, to be quite precise, living with other human beings was such a messy job.

Not that it was so wonderful on board ship – that bastard Bargerone, he was to blame for all this trouble – but at least on a ship everyone had his position, his station, and there were rules to keep him to it, and punish him if he did not keep to it. Perhaps that was the secret of the exploring spirit. Yes, perhaps that had always been the knowledge in the hearts of the other great explorers! Taxing though the unknown realms were, they held no dangers like those that lurked in the breast of friends and family. Better the devils you don't know, than those that know you!

He headed for home in fine angry contentment. Hadn't he always thought that things would turn out like this!

When the Master Explorer had left his office, Sir Mihaly Pasztor drained his glass, set it down, and walked heavily over to the door of his small adjourning room. He opened it.

A young man sat in the large cupped hand of a chair, smoking a mescahale as if he would eat it. He was of willowy build, with a neat beard that made him look older than his eighteen years. His usually intelligent face, as he turned it now in a mute question towards Mihaly, was merely heavy and glum.

"Your father has gone, Aylmer," Mihaly said.

"I recognized his voice. He sounded all overwrought as usual."

They moved back into the office.

Aylmer slipped his mescahale into the disposer on the desk and asked, "What was he after? Anything to do with me?"

"Not really. He wanted me to get him aboard the *Gansas*."

Their eyes met. The young sullen face began to smile. Together, they burst into laughter.

"Like son, like father! You didn't tell him, I hope, that I had come with an exactly similar request?"

"Of course not. He had enough to be unhappy about for one day." As he spoke, Mihaly rummaged in his desk. "Now don't be offended if I push you off fast, young man, but I have a lot of work to do. You are sure that you still want to join the Exploration Corps?"

"You know I do, Uncle Mihaly. I feel I cannot stay on Earth any more. My parents have made that impossible for me, at least for the present. I want to get out into space, away."

Mihaly nodded sympathetically. He'd heard the same sentiments so often, and never discouraged them, if only because he once thought that way himself. When you were young you never realized that there was no "away", only – even in the most distant galaxy – endless locations haunted by the self. He laid out some documents on the top of the desk.

111

"These are the various papers you will need. A friend of mine, Bryant Lattimore of the USGN Flight Advice, has explained things to David Pestalozzi, who will captain the *Gansas* on this run. Because your father is well known, it has been thought wiser to have you ship under an assumed name. Accordingly, you will be known as Samuel Melmoth. I hope you won't mind that?"

"Why should I mind? I'm very grateful for all you have done, and I have no particular fondness for my own name."

He clenched his fists above his head and beamed with triumph.

How easy it was to be excited when you were young, Mihaly thought. How hard for real friendship to spring up between two different generations — one could communicate, but it was often like two different species signalling to each other across a gulf.

"What happened to that girl you were mixed up with?" he asked.

"Oh, her!" The sour look returned for a moment. "She was a dead loss."

"I hope you'll forgive my curiosity, Aylmer, but was she not the cause of your being turned out of your father's house? What did the two of you do that your father regarded as so unforgiveable?"

Aylmer looked restless.

"Come, you can tell me, surely," Mihaly said, with impatience. "I am a broadminded man, a man of the world, nothing like your father."

Aylmer smiled. "That's funny, I always thought that in many ways you and father were rather alike. For instance, you have this background of space travel; and then neither of you likes the hygienic synthetic foods and you still eat old-fashioned foods, such as — well, bits of animal cooked." He made a gesture of disgust and said, "But if it satisfies your curiosity, you may as well know that father came in

112

unexpectedly one night on his last leave when I had my girl on my bed. I was kissing her between the thighs when he opened the door. The sight nearly drove him off his nut! Does it shock you too?"

Looking down at his desk, Mihaly shook his head and said, "My dear Aylmer, what shocks me is that I should appear to you like your father. This business of food — can't you see how generation by generation we are getting farther and farther divorced from nature? This craving for synthetic food is one more instance of man's denial of his animal nature. We are a mixture of animal and spirit, and to deny one side of our nature is to impoverish the other."

"The Stone Age men used the same argument, I daresay, to whoever started cooking their food. But we live in the Buzzardian universe now, and must think accordingly. You must see, Uncle, that we've come too far for us to be able to argue any longer about what is 'natural' and what isn't."

"Oh? Why then are you disgusted about my eating 'bits of animal'?"

"Because that is inherently . . . well, it's just disgusting."

"You'd better go, Aylmer, I have the business of handing over my two aliens to the vivisectors. I wish you well."

"Cheer up, Uncle, we'll be bringing you lots more to experiment on!" And with that thoughtless word of encouragement, Aylmer Ainson was stuffing the documents into his pocket, waving, leaving.

CHAPTER TEN

VIEWED from space on an accelerated time scale, Earth and its peoples might have been taken for one organism. Occasionally the organism would have a convulsion. Moving like microbes down arteries, the human specks would slide down their traffic lanes and converge on various points on the globe until those points began to look like sores on the cuticle of the sphere.

The inflammation would grow, would seem to be a mere diseased confusion, until a change took place. The specks would draw back from a central object, producing a semblance of orderliness. This central object would stand out like a pustule, a stormhead of infection. Then it would burst, or appear to burst, and fly outwards. As if some intolerable pressure had thus been relieved, the people that resembled specks to the cosmic observer would now disperse, possibly to reassemble later at another seat of infection. Meanwhile, the ejected blob of matter hurtled outwards – making the cosmic eye duck out of the way and attend to its own business.

This particular blob of ejected matter bore the name *S.S. Gansas* engraved in glucinated beryllium letters three yards tall on her bows. Once clear of the platter of the solar system, however, the name became scarcely legible even to the most hypothetical observer, for the ship entered TP flight.

Transponential is one of those ideas that have hung on the fringes of man's mind since he first found tongue to express himself, and probably before; almost certainly before, since it is the least puissant who dream most fervently of omnipotence. For, expressed semantically, transponential flight reveals itself as the very opposite of travel; it causes the ship to stand still and the universe to move in the desired direction.

Or perhaps it was explained more accurately by Dr. Chosissy in his World Congress Lecture of 2033, when he said, "However surprising it may seem to those of us brought up in the cosy certainty of Einsteinian physics, the variable factor in the new Buzzardian equations proves to be the universe. Distance may be said to be annihilated. We recognize at last that distance is only a mathematical concept having no real existence in the Buzzardian universe. During TP flight, it is no longer possible to say that the universe surrounds the starship. More accurately, we should say that the starship surrounds the universe." The ancient dreams of power had been realized, and the mountain came obediently to Mahommet.

Cheerfully unaware of the unfair advantage he had over the universe, Hank Quilter was trading tales of his last leave with his new messmates.

"You certainly have all the luck, Hank," said a man whose permanent sugary grin had earned him the name of Honeybunch. "I'd really envy you that girl if I didn't think you were making up half those stories about her."

"If you won't take my word, I'm quite prepared to beat you up till you do," Quilter said.

"Truth through violence!" someone laughed.

"Show me a better way," Quilter said, grinning in turn. Since what he had told them contained very little exaggeration, he was content to have them doubt his word; had he been lying, it would have been a different matter.

"Tell you another funny thing happened to me," he

115

said. "Day before I got to the ship, I got a letter from a guy who messed with me on the *Mariestopes*, nice enough guy called Walthamstone, a Britisher. His first night earth-side, he got drunk and did a spot of housebreaking. The cops caught him at it and sent him down for a term. The way he put it, it sounds he was a bit psychotic at the time. Anyhow, in the jug he meets a pansy, and this pansy turns old Walthamstone the same way – works on him, you know, and turns him the same way! So when they're released, Wal goes to live with this queen in Ghettoville. Now it seems they're good as married!"

Quilter burst into laughter at the thought of it.

A bearded youngster who had not spoken yet, name of Samuel Melmoth, said quietly, "That doesn't seem very funny to me. We all need love of some sort, as your earlier stories prove. I should have thought your friend deserved some pity."

Quilter stopped laughing and looked at Melmoth. He wiped his mouth on his hand.

"What are you trying to give me, Mac? I'm only laughing at the odd things that happen to people. And why should Wally need your goddamned pity? He had a free choice, didn't he? He could do what he liked when he came out of jug, couldn't he?"

Melmoth began to look as stubborn and hurt as his father who bore a different name.

"By what you say, he was seduced."

"Okay, okay, he was seduced. Now you tell me if we aren't all seduced at some time or other in some way or other. That's when our principles are betrayed, isn't it? But if our principles were stronger, then we wouldn't give in, would we? So what happens to Wal is his own look out."

"But if he'd had some friends —"

"It's got nothing to do with friends or seducers or enemies or anything else. That's what I'm saying. It's

116

Wal's own look out. Anything that happens to us is our own responsibility."

"Ah, now, that's a load of garbage," Honeybunch protested.

"You're all sick, that's your trouble," Quilter said.

"Honeybunch is right," Melmoth said. "We all start out in life with more trouble than we can sort out all our days."

"Look, feller, nobody asked your opinion in the first place. Speak for yourself," Quilter said.

"I am."

"Well, kindly refrain from opening your gob on my behalf. I bear my own woes on my own back, and furthermore I believe man possesses free will. I do what I want to do, see?"

At that moment, the speaker system crunched into life: "Attention. Will Rating Hank Quilter, Mess No. 307, Hank Quilter, Mess No. 307, proceed at once to the Flight Advisor's Office on the Scanning Deck, Flight Advisor's Office on the Scanning Deck. That is all."

Grumbling, Quilter moved to obey.

Flight Advisor Bryant Lattimore did not like his office on the Scanning Deck. It was decorated in the modern so-called Ur-Organic style, with walls, floor and ceiling continuously patterned with bas-relief plastic of varied tones. The pattern represented surface crystals of molybdenum oxide under a magnification of 75,000. It was designed to put him in harmony with the Buzzardian universe.

Flight Advisor Bryant Lattimore did like his job.

When the knock came at his door, and Rating Quilter entered, Lattimore nodded him amiably to a chair.

"Quilter, you know why we are hitting vacuum. We intend to discover the home planet of the aliens that I believe are popularly known as rhinomen. My particular task is to formulate in advance some of the lines of approach we can use when we have uncovered this planet. Now I happened to flip through the crew lists and came on your name. You were on the *Mariestopes*, were you not, when this first group of rhinomen was discovered?"

"Sir, I was in the Exploration Corps then, sir. I was one of the men who actually came across the creatures. I shot three or four of them as they charged me. You see —"

"This is very interesting, Quilter, but may we just have this a little more slowly?"

Quilter told his story in elaborate and elaborated detail, while Lattimore listened and gazed at the molybdenum crystals in which he was imprisoned and nodded his head and intermittently loosened a speck of dried mucas from inside one of his nostrils.

"You're certain these creatures attacked you?" he asked, removing his spectacles to stare at Quilter.

Quilter hesitated, weighed Lattimore up, and decided on the truth as he saw it.

"Let's say they came towards us, sir. So we let 'em have it without going into committee first."

Lattimore smiled and resumed his spectacles.

When he had dismissed the rating, he pressed a bell and Mrs. Hilary Warhoon appeared. She looked very smart in a flared mock-male with recessed carnation paltroons; the glint in her eyes showed how delighted she was to be loose in the Buzzardian universe.

"Had Quilter anything of interest to say?" she asked, sitting down at the table next to Lattimore.

"Only inadvertently. He's read his newscasts and his poppers, and on the surface his attitude is the civilized one: that we don't know much about the rhinomen, as he calls them, and that we give them the benefit of the doubt until we find whether or not they are glorified hogs. Underneath, and not very far underneath, he *knows* the critters are just big game, and to be shot like big game, because he has shot them like big game. You know, even if it does

118

turn out that they are brilliant thinkers and all that, our relationship with them is going to be precious damn difficult."

"Yes. Because if they are brilliant thinkers, their thought is going to be remarkably different from our thought."

"Check. And not that only. Philosophers who live in mud are not going to cut much ice with Earth; the masses have always been a deal more impressed by mud than by philosophers."

"Fortunately, what the masses think won't affect us out here."

"You think not? Heck, you're the cosmoclectic, Hilary, but I've been in TP before, and I know a strange psychology rules on shipboard. It's like an exaggerated version of Kipling's 'East of Suez . . .', how's it go now? 'Ship me somewheres east of Suez, where the best is like the worst, where there ain't no Ten Commandments. . . .' The best are very like the worst when you step on a planet lying under another sun, Hilary. And you feel that – well, it's a sort of irresponsibility – you feel that you can do anything you like because nobody on Earth will judge you for it: while at the same time, 'just what you like' is naturally part of what the masses of Earth would like to do, had they the licence."

Mrs. Warhoon tapped four pliant fingers on the table.

"You make it sound very sinister."

"Hell, the irrational drives of man are sinister! Don't think I'm generalizing. I've seen this mood come over a man too often. It was probably that that undid Ainson. And I feel it in myself."

"Now I'm afraid I don't see what you mean."

"Don't look so offended. I could *feel* that your Quilter really enjoyed shooting our friends. The thrill of the chase! If I saw a bunch of 'em nipping over the veldt, I wouldn't mind a shot myself."

Mrs. Warhoon's voice was slightly chilled.

"What do you intend to do if we find the ETA home planet?"

"You know what I intend to do: act according to logic and reason. This outfit is for business, not pleasure. But I'm also aware that there's a part of me saying; Lattimore, these creatures don't feel pain; how can anything have a spirit or a soul or be intelligent or appreciate some unimaginable equivalent of Byron's poems or Borodin's Second Symphony if it does not suffer? And I say to myself, whatever gifts it has, if it has not pain, then it is for ever beyond the reach of my comprehension."

"But that is just the challenge, that is why we are having to try to comprehend, that —" She looked attractive with her fists clenched.

"I know all that. But you are talking to me in the voice of intellect," Lattimore said, leaning back in his chair. It was pleasurable shooting Hilary this all-male line. "I'm also hearing a sort of Quilter-voice, a *vox populi*, a cry not only from the heart but from the bowels. It says that whatever talents these critters may have, they are less than buffaloes or zebras or tigers, and the primitive urge comes up in me just as it did in Quilter, and I want to shoot them."

She had eight ruby-tipped fingers drumming on the table now, but she managed to look into his face and laugh.

"You are playing an intellectual game with yourself, Bryant. I'm sure that even the base Quilter offered excuses for his actions. Therefore even he feels guilt for his actions; you, being more intelligent, can savour your guilt beforehand, and so control yourself."

"East of Suez, an intelligent man can find more excuses for himself than a cretin can."

Seeing vexation on her face, he relented.

"As you say, I'm probably playing a game with myself. Or with you."

He placed a hand over her finger-tips as carelessly as if they were molybdenum crystals. She withdrew them.

"I wish to change the topic of conversation, Bryant. I have a suggestion that I think may be fruitful. Do you think you could get me a volunteer?"

"For what?"

"To be marooned on a strange planet."

Back on the strange planet called Earth, the third Politan called Blug Lugug was in a terrible state of mental confusion. He was strapped to a bench with a series of strong canvas straps that passed across what was left of his body. A number of wires and cables ran from machines that stood silent or gargled to themselves on one side of the room and climbed on to his body or into his various orifices. One cable in particular ran from one instrument in particular worked by one man in particular; the man was dressed in a white sort of clothing, and when he moved a lever with his hand, something without meaning happened in the third Politan's brain. This meaningless thing was more awful than anything the third Politan had known existed. He saw now how right the Sacred Cosmopolitan had been when he used to term *bad* to describe these thinlegs. Here was *bad bad bad*: it reared up before him sturdy and strong and hygienic, and gnawed away his intelligence bit by bit.

The something without meaning came again. A gulf opened where there had been something growing, something delightful, memories or promises, who knows?, but something never to be replaced.

One of the thinlegs spoke. Mainly, in gasps, the Politan imitated what had been said: "noneuralresponsethere/either. He/doesnthave/apainresponsein/his/wholebody!"

He still clung to the notion that when they realized he could imitate their speech, they would be intelligent enough to stop the things they were doing. Whatever they were doing, whatever inside their mad little minds they imagined they were doing, they were spoiling his chances of entering the carrion stage; for already they had removed two of his limbs with a saw – from the corner of his misting eyes he watched the bin in which they had been deposited – and since there were no ammp trees here, the possibility of his continuing the cycles of being was remote. Nothingness confronted him.

He cried an imitation of their words but, forgetting their limitations, pushed it high into his upper voice range. The sounds came distorted; his ockpu orifices were clogged with tiny instruments like leeches.

He needed comfort from the Sacred Cosmopolitan, his worshipped father-mother. But the Cosmopolitan had gone, no doubt to the same gradual dismemberment. The grorgs had gone; he caught their almost supersonic cries answering him in lament from a distant part of the room. Then the something without meaning burst over him again, so that he could no longer hear – but what was it that he had been able to . . . been able to what? Something else had gone.

In his dizziness, he saw that a new figure had joined the figures in white. In his dizziness, he thought he recognized the new figure. It was – or it was very like – the figure that had performed the dung ritual a brief time ago.

Now the figure cried something, and through the growing dizziness the Politan tried to cry the same thing back, to show it had recognized him: "Ican'tbeartowatchyou're doingsomethingthatshouldneverbedone!"

But the thinlegs, if it was that specific one, gave no sign of recognition. He covered the front part of his upper head with his hands and went fast from the room, almost as if —

The something without meaning came again, and the white figures all looked eagerly at their instruments.

Tipped far back until his toes were level with his head,

122

the Director of the Exozoo lay in his therapad and sucked a glucose mixture through a teat. He was being calmed by a young men, now a member of the Exploration Corps with an Explorer's certificate, who had once trained under him at the zoo. Gussie Phipps, who had flown in from Macao, offered comfort.

"You're not so tough as you used to be, Sir Mihaly. You ought to change to synthetic foods; they're better for you. Fancy letting a vivisection upset you! How many vivisections have you performed yourself?"

"I know, I know, you needn't remind me. It was just the sight of that particular poor creature there on the stone, slowly being chopped into little bits and not registering anything detectable as pain or fear."

"Which should make it better rather than worse."

"Heavens, I know it should! But it was so darned *unresentful*! I had the feeling for a moment I was in at a preview of how man will treat any intelligent opposition it meets out there." He gestured vaguely towards the patterned ceiling. "Or perhaps I mean that beneath the scientific etiquette of the vivisection bench I heard the savage drums of ancient man, still beating away like mad for a blood-letting session. What is man up to, Gussie?"

"Such an outburst of pessimism is unlike you. We're coming away from the mud, away from the primeval slime, away from the animal, towards the spiritual. We have a long way to go, but —"

"Yes, it's an answer I've often used myself. We may not be very nice now but we'll be nicer at some unspecified future time. But is it true? Oughtn't we to have stayed in the mud? Mightn't it be more healthy and sane down there? And are we just giving ourselves excuses to carry on as we always did? Think how many primitive rites are still with us in a thin disguise: vivisection, giving in marriage, cosmetics, hunting, wars, circumcision – no, I don't want to think of any more. When we do make an

123

advance, it's in a ghastly false direction – like the synth food fad, inspired by last century's dietary madnesses and thrombosis scares. It's time I retired, Gussie, got away while I'm not too aged, moved to some simpler clime where the sun shines. I've always believed that the amount of thought that goes on inside a man's head is in inverse proportion to the amount of sunshine that goes on outside it."

The door globe chimed.

"I'm expecting nobody," Pasztor said, with an irritability he rarely showed. "Go and see who it is for me, Gussie, and shoo them away. I want to hear all about Macao from you."

Phipps disappeared, to return with Enid Ainson, weeping.

Nipping with momentary savagery on the end of his glucose teat, Pasztor jacked himself into a less relaxed position and stuck a leg out of the therapad.

"It's Bruce, Mihaly!" Enid cried. "Bruce has disappeared. I'm sure he's drowned himself. Oh Mihaly, he's been so difficult! What can I do?"

"When did you last see him?"

"He couldn't stand the disgrace of being turned down for the *Gansas*. I know he's drowned himself. He often threatened he would."

"When did you last see him, Enid?"

"Whatever shall I do? I must let poor Aylmer know!"

Pasztor climbed out of the pad. He gripped Phipps' elbow as he moved towards the technivision.

"We'll have to hear about Macao some other time, Gussie," he said.

He began to technicall the police, while Enid wept in a businesslike way behind him.

Bruce Ainson was already a fair distance beyond the reach of Earth police.

On the day after the *Gansas* was ejected into space, a much less publicized flight began. Blasting from a small operational spaceport on the east coast of England, a systemship started its long haul across the ecliptic. Systemships were an altogether different sort of spaceship from the starships. They carried no TP drive. They fuelled on ions, consuming most of their bulk as they travelled. They were built for duties within the solar system only, and most of them that left Britain nowadays were military craft.

The *I.S. Brunner* was no exception. It was a trooper, packed to the hull with reinforcements for the Anglo-Brazilian war on Charon. Among those reinforcements was an ageing and troubled nonentity named B. Ainson, who had been mustered as a clerk.

That sullen outcast of the solar family, Charon, known generally to soldiers as the Deep Freeze Planet, had been discovered telescopically by the Wilkins-Pressman Lunar Observatory almost two decades before it was visited by man. The First Charon Expedition (on which was a brilliant young Hungarian dramatist and biologist named Mihaly Pasztor) discovered it to be the father of all billiard balls, a globe some three hundred miles in diameter (307·558 miles, according to the latest edition of the Brazilian Military Manual, 309·567 miles according to its British equivalent). This globe was without feature, its surface smooth in texture, white in colour, slippery and almost without chemical properties. It was hard, but not extremely hard. It could be bored into with high-speed drills.

To say that Charon had no atmosphere was inaccurate. The smooth white surface was the atmosphere, frozen out over the long and unspeakably tedious eons during which Charon, a travelling morgue without benefit of bones, trundled its bulk about its orbit, connected by what hardly seemed more than coincidence with a first magni-

125

tude star called Sol. When the atmosphere was dug and analysed, it was found to consist of a mixture of inert gasses packed together into a form unknown to, and un-reproducible in, Earth's laboratories. Somewhere below this surface, seismographic reports indicated, was the real Charon: a rocky and pulseless heart two hundred miles across.

The Deep Freeze Planet was an ideal place on which to hold wars.

Despite their excellent effect on trade, wars have a deleterious effect on the human body; so they became, during the second decade of the twenty-first century, codified, regulated, umpired, as much subject to skill as a baseball game or to law as a judge's table talk. Because Earth was very crowded, wars were banished to Charon. There, the globe had been marked out with tremendous lines of latitude and longitude, like a celestial draughts board.

Earth was by no means peacefully inclined. In con-sequence, there were frequently waiting lists for space on Charon, the lists consisting mainly of belligerent nations who wished to book regions about the equator, where the light for fighting was slightly better. The Anglo-Brazilian war occupied Sectors 159–260, adjacent to the current Javanese-Guinean conflict, and had been dragging on since the year 1999. A Contained Conflict it was called.

The rules of Contained Conflict were many and in-volved. For instance, the weapons of destruction were rigidly defined. And certain highly qualified social ranks – who might bring their side unfair advantages – were for-bidden on Charon. Penalties for breaking such rules were very high. And, for all the precautions that were taken, casualties among combatants were also high.

In consequence, the flower of English youth, to say nothing of blooms of a blowsier age, were needed on Charon; Bruce Ainson had taken advantage of that fact to enlist as a man without social rank and to slip quietly out of the public eye. A century earlier, he would probably have joined the Foreign Legion.

As the little ion-driven trooper carried him now over the ten light hours that separated Earth and Charon, he might, had he known of it, have reflected with contempt on Sir Mihaly's glib remark that the amount of thought in a man's head is in inverse proportion to the amount of sun outside it. He might have so reflected, if only the *Brunner* permitted reflection among the men packed between its decks head to tail; but Ainson, together with all his companions, went out to the Deep Freeze Planet in deep freeze.

CHAPTER ELEVEN

ONE of the ways – if you were an intellectual – of proving you were not an intellectual was to stroll up and down the Scanning Deck with the sleeves of your tunic rolled untidily to the elbow. You put one of the big new corky mescahales between your lips, and you strolled up and down laughing heartily at your own jokes or at those of your companion. That way, the ratings who came up here for a gaze at the universe could see for themselves that you were human.

The faulty ingredient in this prescription, Lattimore thought, was his current companion, Marcel Gleet, the Second Navigation Officer. It would have constituted a major solecism, almost a solar solecism, to have laughed at what Gleet said. Gleet was wedded to seriousness, and the marriage was much like a funeral.

"... would seem a substantial possibility," he was saying, "that the star cluster, the co-ordinates of which I have just mentioned, may be the home of our alien species. There are six stars in the cluster having between them some fifteen orbiting planets. I was talking with Mellor of Geocred last watch, and he infers that as many as six of them are likely to prove Earth-type."

One certainly couldn't laugh at that, Lattimore thought, though there were several crew about on the deck, not a few of them laughing – mainly at Mrs. Warhoon's notice, which was pinned conspicuously to the main notice board.

"Since all of these six Earth-type bodies," Gleet continued, "are within two to three light years of Clementina, they would seem to constitute a reasonable area in which to pursue our search. A further advantage is that the six bodies are all within light days of each other, an immense help with regard to flight promptitude."

At least a chuckle of agreement might be inserted there.

Gleet continued his discourse, but the chime of a watch bell reminded him of the reason for his coming up to the Scanning Deck, and he moved away in the direction of the Navigation Bay. Lattimore turned to one of the deep oval ports, and gazed out through the hull of the ship while he listened to the comments of a group of three men behind him.

" 'Contribution to the future of mankind!' That I like!" one of them exclaimed, reading from the announcement.

"Yes, but you notice that after that appeal to your better nature, they cover themselves by offering you a pension for life," said one of his companions.

"It would have to be higher stakes than that to get me to maroon myself on an alien planet for five years," the third said.

"I'd chip in too, just to get rid of you," said the first.

128

Lattimore nodded to his ghostly reflection as the ancient form of badinage by insult ran its predictable course. He often wondered at that accepted method of verbal assault which passed for wit; no doubt it was a way of sublimating a man's hatred for his fellows; what else could it be? He was not at all perturbed at the comments passed on Mrs. Warhoon's notice; frigid she might be, but he thought she had a good idea there; because there were many varieties of men, her notice would eventually bear fruit.

He stared at the universe which the *Gansas*, in a Buzzardian way, was currently surrounding. Against a uterine blackness stood a number of close and fuzzy bars of light. It was like a drunken fly's close-up view of a comb, lacking definition and forming an affront to the optic nerve.

But, as the scientists pointed out, the human optic nerve was not adjusted to reality. Because the true nature of the universe could only be glimpsed through the transponential equations, it followed that this fuzzy grill (which made one feel, come to think of it, like a minor crustacean with the baleen of a blue whale grinning down at one) was what the stars "really" looked like. Plato, reflected Lattimore, thou shouldst be living at this hour! He swung away and contrived to turn his thoughts similarly away towards the thought of food.

Say what you liked, there was nothing like a good synthetic stew for calling armistice between a man and his universe.

"But, Mihaly," Enid Ainson was saying, "Mihaly, for years – since Bruce first introduced me to you, I've thought you were secretly attracted to me. I mean the way you looked at me. And when you consented to be Aylmer's godfather – I mean you've always led me to think. ..." She pressed her hands together. "And you were only

129

amusing yourself. . . ."

He was drawn up very formally, a cliff against the tide of her pathos.

"Perhaps I have a naturally chivalrous attitude to ladies, Enid, but you have read too much into it. What can I do but thank you deeply for your flattering suggestion, but really. . . ."

Suddenly she jerked her head up. She had eaten enough at the apple of humiliation; it was time to let anger have its turn. Imperiously she gestured at him.

"You need say no more. I will tell you only that the thought of you and your imagined fondness – how often I foolishly imagined that it was only your friendship with Bruce that kept you from making advances towards me! – your hollow fondness has been the only factor keeping me sane over these last few impossible years."

"Come, I am certain you exaggerate —"

"I am talking! I see now that all your airs and graces, all this phoney Hungarian glamour you put on, they all mean nothing. You are just a false front, Mihaly, a romantic who dislikes romances, a – a ladies' man who is afraid of ladies. Good-bye to you, Mihaly, and damn you! Through you I have lost both my husband and my son."

The door slammed behind her.

They had been talking in the hall. Mihaly put his hands up to his burning cheeks. He was shaking. He averted his eyes from the sight of himself in the mirror.

The terrible thing was, that without having the least interest in Enid physically, he had admired her spirit and, knowing what a difficult man Bruce was behind the scenes, he had indeed encouraged her with warm glances and occasional pressures of the hand – purely to illustrate to her that someone was capable of seeing her virtues. Ah, beware, indeed beware of pity!

"Darling, has she gone?"

He heard the tiny summoning voice of his mistress from

the living room. Doubtless she would have eavesdropped on the scene with Enid. Without eagerness, he went to hear what she had to say about it all. There was no doubt that the charming Ah Chi, after her painting holiday in the Persian Gulf or wherever she had been, would be horribly inquisitive over the whole incident.

It was only a watch after Bryant Lattimore had felt like a minor crustacean that Mrs. Warhoon got a volunteer. The discovery sent her in a flutter into the heart of the molybdenum crystal belt. Lattimore quickly took the chance to seize her by her fleshy upper arms.

"Steady now, Hilary! I hate to see a pretty cosmoclectician in a tizzy. So you wanted a volunteer, so you've got him; now go ahead and give him the pitch."

Mrs. Warhoon freed herself, though not without getting appetizingly disarranged. What strong brutes men were! Heaven alone knew what this one would be like when he got metaphorically east of Suez at next planetfall. Well, at least a woman had her own defences: she could always give in.

"This volunteer is rather special, Mr. Lattimore. Does the name Samuel Melmoth mean anything to you?"

"Not a thing. No, wait! Ye gods and little fishes! It's Ainson's son! You mean *he's* volunteered?"

"He has managed to make himself rather unpopular down on the messdeck, and in consequence feels rather anti-social. A friend of his called Quilter gave him a black eye."

"Quilter again, eh? Likely leader material there; I must speak to the captain about him."

"I'd like you to come and stand by me while I brief this young Ainson, if you aren't too busy."

"Hilary, I'd stand by you at any time."

The Ur-Organic style (like all art movement labels, the name was inaccurate to the point of meaninglessness) had

131

perpetrated a nasty whimsy in Mrs. Warhoon's office. She and Lattimore stepped into a popinjay's heart. Under a magnification of 200,000, the fibrous tissue ran and knotted in bas-relief over ceiling and floor as well as walls. In the middle of it, lonely, green about one eye, sat Aylmer Ainson, his head indistinct against a galaxy of striated aortal muscle. He stood when Mrs. Warhoon and Lattimore entered.

Poor little devil, thought Lattimore. The lady here is somewhat up a gum tree in concluding that it was anything so simple as a black eye that led this boy to want to maroon himself on a strange planet. His whole history – and his parents' history, and so their parents' history, and so back to those first deluded dimwits who decided that animal life wasn't good enough for them – everything has led to this act of his; the black eye was just a clincher. And who would say, who could be a fly-sized god and see it all, that the clincher was accidental? Maybe the poor kid had to provoke the assault to reassure himself that the outside world was the aggressor.

Somewhere, Lattimore thought (but with as much complacency as trepidation, as he realized) my upbringing took the wrong turning, or I would not diagnose so much meaning from the hangdog-proud way this kiddie stood up for us.

"Sit down, Mr. Melmoth," Mrs. Warhoon said, in a pleasant voice Lattimore found unpleasant. "This is the Flight Advisor, Mr. Lattimore. He knows as well as anyone the communication problems you will be up against, and can give you pointers on the subject."

"How do you do, sir," young Ainson said, smiling round his puffy eye.

"Firstly, the larger programme," said Mrs. Warhoon, and chose a military phrase with winsome self-consciousness, "just to put you in the picture, as they say. When we come out of TP flight, we shall be in a star cluster that contains at least fifteen planets, of which six, to judge by a remote technivisual survey conducted by the *Marie-stopes*, have Earth-type atmospheres. Our aliens, as you know, were found beside a space vehicle – whether it belonged to them or to an allied species, we hope to determine soon. But its suggests that we may find space flight established in this cluster. In that case we shall need to survey all inhabited planets. It was planned before we left Earth that on the first such planet we should deposit an unmanned observation post. Since then, however, I have had a further idea, which Captain Pestalozzi has agreed to let me carry out.

"My idea is simply to leave a volunteer with the observation post. Since we could furnish him with provisions and food synthesizers, and the natives, as we know by our captive specimens, will not be hostile, such a volunteer would be quite secure from danger. As we now see, you have consented to be that volunteer."

Safe in the blown-up popinjay heart, they all smiled at each other.

But does he detect, Lattimore asked himself, the lie in Mrs. Warhoon's words? Who knows yet what hells these rhinomen may create on their home ground, who knows if there isn't some man-devouring form of farmer who uses the rhinomen as greedily as we use the Improved Danish Landrace pig? And of course the old Lattimoronic question, who knows what hells this latter day Saint Anthony will create for himself in his alien wilderness? That ill wind cannot be sheltered from, but the others can.

"And, naturally, we will see you are well-armed," he said, aware by Mrs. Warhoon's glance that she saw the remark as a minor betrayal.

Compressing her lips, she turned back to Ainson.

"Now to what we expect you to do. We expect you to learn to communicate with the aliens."

"But the experts couldn't do that on Earth. How do you

133

expect me —"

"We shall train you, Mr. Melmoth. There are nine whole ship's days before we break out of TP, and much can be learnt in that time. On Earth, it may have been that an impossible task was attempted; on the aliens' home planet, when we can see them in their own context, the task will be much lighter. Indeed, the aliens should be very much more communicative in their own environment. We think that probably the wonders of Earth, the size of our starships, and so on, may have partly paralysed their responses.

"As you may know, we had six alien bodies on which thorough dissections were performed. Our specimens were of different ages, some young, some old. From analysis of their bone tissue, we think they may attain ages of some hundreds of years; their insusceptibility to pain tends to support this theory. If this is so, then it should follow that they would have protracted childhoods.

"Now I get to my next point. The learning time of any species is in its early days, its babydays, and wherever we go in the galaxy we can expect to find the same rule applying. Children on Earth who through some misadventure learn no language are at twelve or thirteen too old to learn one. This has been proved many times with babies, for instance, in India, who have been tended by monkeys or wolves. Once the time of childhood is past, they are past acquiring the gift of speech.

"So I have reasoned, Mr. Melmoth, that the only time that the aliens might be able to learn our tongue would be during their early years. It will be your job to live as close as you possibly can to one such infant alien.

"It may be – we don't deny it – that it will prove impossible to communicate with these creatures. But the proof must be conclusive. After we have left you, we shall go to investigate the other planets in the cluster; no doubt we shall capture a group of the aliens and take them back to Earth, or even establish a base on one of the other planets, but that will have to wait on local conditions. Meanwhile, you will be my Number One project."

For a moment, Aylmer said nothing. He was thinking, in fact, about the winds of chance, and how wildly they blew. Only a brief while ago he was so stickily involved in the web of personal relationships formed by his father, his mother, his girl, and, to a lesser degree, his uncle Mihaly. Now that he was miraculously free, there was one question in particular he wanted to ask: "How long will you be leaving me on this planet?"

"Well, it will be for no longer than a year, that I promise," Mrs. Warhoon told him, and was relieved to see his frown dissolve. They all smiled at each other again, though both men looked ill at ease.

"How does all that sound to you?" Mrs. Warhoon asked Aylmer Ainson sympathetically.

For heck sake tell her that you realize you have stuck your neck out too far to stomach, thought Lattimore, toying with a metaphor he had mixed some days earlier. Tell her that you can't afford to pay such a high price for the catharsis you need. Or look at me for assistance and I'll put in a word for you.

The boy did look at Lattimore, but there were pride and excitement rather than appeal in the glance.

Okay, Lattimore thought, so my diagnosis was a complete cock-up. So he's a hero rather than a couch case. A man is his own responsibility.

"I feel very honoured to be given such an assignment," Aylmer Ainson said.

CHAPTER TWELVE

LIKE a dog that has been harshly spoken to, the universe had resumed its customary position. No longer did it cause the *Gansas* to surround it. Instead, it surrounded the big ship, and the big ship sat on the planet with its nose in the air.

In honour of the ship's captain, the planet had been christened Pestalozzi – though as Navigator Gleet had pointed out there were more pleasant names.

Everything on Pestalozzi was fine.

Its air contained the right admixture of oxygen at ground level, and lacked any vapours that might offend terrestrial lungs. Even better, it harboured – and they had Med Section's word for it – no bacterium or virus that Med Section could not cope with if necessary.

The *Gansas* had landed near the equator. The midday temperature had not risen above twenty degrees Celsius, but at night it had not sunk below nine degrees.

The period of axial revolution corresponded conveniently with Earth's, taking a notch over twenty-four hours and nine minutes. Which meant that a point on the equator would be travelling faster than an equivalent point on Earth, for one great disadvantage about Pestalozzi was that it was a world with considerable mass.

Rest periods had been ordered after midday mess. Most

of the crew had voluntarily started slimming. For seven stone weaklings on Pestalozzi weighed twenty-one stones at the equator.

There were compensations for this crippling tripling, chief among which was the discovery of the aliens.

When it had sat on its haunches smelling the air, observing solar emissions, ground radioactivity, magnastic bathytherms, and other phenomena, for two days, the *Gansas* emitted small snooper craft. As well as having an exploratory function, these flights were calculated to relieve cosmophobia.

Honeybunch sat at the controls of one of these craft, flying according to Lattimore's instructions. Lattimore was in a state of great excitement, which communicated itself to the rating sitting next to him, Hank Quilter. They both gripped the rail and stared at the tawny lands rippling beneath them like the flank of a vast and vastly galloping beast. . . .

A beast we'll learn to tame and ride, thought Lattimore, trying to analyse the choking sensation in his breast. This is what that whole school of minor writers was fumbling to say last century before space travel even began, and, ye gods and little fishes, they had more than was acknowledged. Because this is the genuine and only thing, to feel the squeeze in your cells of a different gravity, to ride over a ground innocent of all thought of man, to be the first that ever burst.

It was like getting your childhood back, a big savage childhood; once, long ago, you'd gone behind the lavender bushes at the bottom of the garden and had stepped into terra incognita. Here it was again, and every stalk of grass a lavender bush.

He checked himself.

"Hover," he ordered. "Alien life ahead."

They hovered, and beneath them a broad and lazy river was fringed with salad beds. In isolated groups the rhinomen worked or sheltered behind trees.

Lattimore and Quilter looked at each other.

"Set her down," Lattimore ordered.

Honeybunch set her down more daintily than he had ever handled woman.

"Better have your rifles in case there's trouble," Lattimore said.

They picked up their rifles and climbed with care to the ground. Ankles were easily broken at current weights, despite the hastily devised supports that they all wore to thigh height under their trousers.

A line of trees stood about eighty yards west of them. The three men headed for the trees, picking their way through rows of cultivated plants that resembled bolting lettuce, except that their leaves were as large and coarse as rhubarb leaves.

The trees were enormous, but notable chiefly for what looked like malformation of their trunks. They swelled and spread, each of them double lobed; they approximated the shape of the aliens with their plump bodies and two sharp heads. From their crests, aerial roots tapered, many of them, like crude fingers. The foliage bristling on their topknots grew in a sort of stiff turbulence, so that again Lattimore felt the shiver of wonder; here was something his weary intellect had not contemplated before.

As the three moved towards these trees, rifles half-raised in traditional gesture, four-winged birds – butterflies the size of eagles – clattered out of the tousled foliage, circled, and made away towards the low hills on the far side of the river. Beneath the trees, half a dozen rhinomen stood to watch the men approach. Their smell was familiar to Lattimore. He released the safety button of his rifle.

"I didn't realise they were so big," Honeybunch said softly. "Are they going to charge us? We can't run – hadn't we better get back to the snooper?"

138

"They're all ready to run," Quilter said. He wiped his wet lips with his hand.

Lattimore had judged that the mildly swivelling heads of the aliens indicated no more than curiosity, but he welcomed this token that Quilter felt as much in control of the situation as he did.

"Keep walking, Honeybunch," he said.

But Honeybunch had glanced back over his shoulder at their craft. He let out a cry.

"Hey, they're attacking from the rear!"

Seven of the aliens, two of them big chaps with grey hides, approached the snooper from behind, were moving towards it inquisitively, were only a few yards from it. Honeybunch lugged the rifle up to his hips and fired.

His first shot missed. The second found a target. The men heard the californium slug hit with a force equivalent to seventeen tons of T.N.T. One of the big grey fellows heeled over, a crater torn in the smooth terrain of his back.

The other creatures moved to their companion as Honeybunch's rifle came up again.

"Hold your fire!" Lattimore said.

His voice was cut off by the roar of Quilter's rifle on his left. Ahead, one of the smaller aliens burst, a head and shoulders blown away.

Unknown tendons in Lattimore's neck and face tightened. He saw the rest of the stupid things standing there, nonplussed, but giving no appearance of fear or anger, certainly showing no inclination to run. They could feel nothing! If they had not sense enough to see the power of men, they should be taught it. There wasn't a species living that didn't know about man and his fire-power. What were they good for but to serve as targets?

Lattimore brought his rifle up. It was a short mechanism with collapsible butt, semi-silenced, semi-recoilless, firing a 0·5 slug on single or automatic. It went off just as Quilter fired again.

They stood there shoulder to shoulder, firing until the seven aliens were blown asunder. Now Honeybunch was crying for them to stop. Lattimore and Quilter recognized each other's expressions.

"If we went up in the snooper and flew low, we might throw a scare into them and get a moving target," Lattimore said. He polished up his spectacles, which had misted, on the front of his shirt.

Quilter wiped his dry lips on the back of his hand.

"Somebody ought to teach those slugs how to run," he agreed.

Mrs. Warhoon, meanwhile, stood speechless before perfection. She had been invited aboard the captain's snooper, and they had descended to investigate what looked like an untidy cluster of ruins in the interior of the equatorial continent.

There they had found proof of the aliens' intellectual status. There were the mines, the foundries, the refineries, the factories, the laboratories, the launching pads – all domesticated down to the level of a cottage industry. The entire industrial process had turned into a folk art; the spaceships were homespun. They knew then, as they walked unmolested among the snorting aliens, that they were in the midst of an immemorial race. Here was an antiquity beyond the imagining of man.

Captain Pestalozzi had stopped and lit a mescahale.

"Degenerate," he had said. "A race in decline, that's obvious."

"I don't think anything is obvious. We are too far from Earth for anything to be obvious." Mrs. Warhoon said.

"You've only got to look at the things," the captain had replied. He had little sympathy for Mrs. Warhoon;

she was too knowledgeable, and when she wandered away from his party, he felt nothing but a slight relief.

It was then that she had stumbled on perfection.

The few buildings were scattered, and informal rather than negligible architecturally. All walls sloped inwards towards curving roofs; they were built either of bricks or precision-shaped stones, both materials being wrought to interlock, so that no mortar or cement was used. Whether this was a style dictated by the 3G gravity or by artistic whim, Mrs. Warhoon was content to leave undecided until later. She disliked the sort of uninformed conclusions jumped to by the captain. With the thought of him bearing on her mind, she entered one of the buildings no more elaborate than its neighbours, and there the statue stood.

It was perfection.

But perfection is a cold word. This had the warmth as well as the aloofness of achievement.

Her throat constricted, she walked round it.

God knew what it was doing standing in a stinking shack.

It was a statue of one of the aliens. She did not need telling it had also been wrought by one of them. What she did need telling was whether the work had been done yesterday or thirty-six centuries ago. After a while, when this thought had made the circuit of her brain several times, it registered on her attention, and she realized why she had postulated thirty-six centuries. That would be the age of the Egyptian XVIIIth Dynasty statue of a seated figure she often went to contemplate in the British Museum. This work, carved like the other out of a dark granite, had some of the same qualities.

The alien stood on his six limbs, in perfect balance, one of his pointed heads a shade more elevated than the other. Between the catenary curve of his spine and the parabola of his belly lay the great symmetrical boat of his body. She felt curiously humble to be in the room with him; for

141

this was beauty, and for the first time she held in the hollow of her understanding a knowledge of what beauty was: the reconciliation between humanity and geometry, between the personal and the impersonal, between the spirit and the body.

Now Mrs. Warhoon shook inside her mock-male. She saw a lot of things which, because they were important, she did not wildly want to see.

She saw that here was a civilized race that had come to its maturity by a very different path from man's. For this race from the start and continuously (or without more than a brief intermission) had never been in conflict with nature and the natural scene that sustained it. It had remained in rapport, undivorced. Consequently, its struggle towards the sort of abilities living in this shaped granite – ah, but the philosopher and the sculptor, the man of the spirit and the man with the instrument, had been one here! – was the struggle with its natural repose (torpor, many would have said); while man's struggle had in the main been an outward struggle, against forces that he saw as being in opposition to him.

As surely and simply as Mrs. Warhoon saw all this, and before she embellished it for her report, she saw that mankind could not fail to misunderstand this lifeform: for here was an equipoise that would, could, neither oppose nor flee from him. As this was a race without pain, as it was a race without fear, it would remain alien to man.

She had her arm about the flank of the statue, her temple resting on its polished side.

She wept.

For all these perceptions – which came to her on the wing as she walked once round the figure – were mainly intellectual, and fled as they came. In their place grew a womanly perception she could less easily, afterwards, deny.

She perceived the humanity in the statue. It was this

142

humanity that had reminded her of the Egyptian statue. She saw that although this was an abstraction, yet it retained humanity, or the quality humans call humanity; and it was something that mankind had lost and might have retained. She wept for the loss: her loss, everyone's loss.

It was then that the distant shouts broke in on her melancholy. Shots followed, and then the whistles and wails of aliens. Captain Pestalozzi was having or creating trouble.

Wearily, she stood up and brushed her hair off her forehead. She told herself she was being silly. Without looking again at the figure, she went to the door of the building.

Four ship's days later, the *Gansas* was ready to move on to the next planet.

After the experiences of the first day, despite all that a rather hysterical Mrs. Warhoon could say, it was generally agreed that the aliens were a degenerate form of life, if anything rather worse than animals, and were therefore fair game for the natural high spirits of the men. For a day or two, a little hunting could hurt no one.

True, it soon became obvious from planetary sweeps that Pestalozzi harboured only a few hundred thousand of the large sexipeds, congregating round wallows and artificially created swamps; and these began to show evidence that they resented the old Adam in their Eden. But several specimens were captured and penned aboard the *Gansas*; Mrs. Warhoon's statue was likewise collected, and a number of artifacts of a miscellaneous nature, and specimens of plant life.

Disappointingly, there were few other lifeforms on the planet; several varieties of bird, six-legged rodents, lizards, armour-plated flies, fish and crustacea in the rivers and oceans, an interesting shrew discovered in the Arctic regions that seemed to be an exception to the rule that small warm-blooded animals could not survive in such conditions. Little else. Methodically, the Exo Section stocked up the ship.

They were ready to embark on the next leg of their reconnaissance.

Mrs. Warhoon went with the ship's padre, the ship's adjutant, Lattimore, and Quilter (who had just been promoted to a new post as Lattimore's assistant) to say good-bye to Samuel Melmoth, alias Aylmer Ainson, in his stockade.

"I just hope he's going to be all right," Mrs. Warhoon said.

"Stop worrying. He's got enough ammunition here to shoot every living thing on the planet," Lattimore said. He was irritated by his new success with the woman. Ever since the first day of Pestalozzi when she had suddenly become chummy and climbed into his bed, Hilary had been weepy and unsettled. Lattimore reckoned he was easy-going enough where women were concerned, but he like some token that his attentions had a benevolent effect.

He stood by the gate of the stockade, resting on his thigh crutches and feeling vaguely aggrieved with the universe. The others could say farewell to young Ainson. Speaking for himself, he had had enough of the Ainsons.

The stockade was of reinforced wire net. It formed a wall eight feet high about two square acres of ground. A stream ran through the ground. Some damage had been done in the way of trampling down vegetation and shattering trees by the labour force detailed to erect the stockade, but apart from that the area represented a typical bit of Pestalozzi country. By the rivulet was a wallow which led to one of the low native houses. Salad and vegetable beds lay by the wallow, and the whole patch was sheltered rather delightfully by the outrageous trees.

Beyond the trees stood the automatic observation post,

its radio mast rising gracefully into the air. Next to it was the eight-roomed building designed from prefabricated parts for Ainson's residence. Two of the rooms constituted his living space; the others contained all the apparatus he would need for recording and interpreting the alien language, an armoury, medical and other supplies, the power plant, and the food synthesizer, which could be fed water, soil, rock, anything, and would turn them into nourishment.

Beyond the works of man, keeping apart and considerably abashed, sat an adult female alien and her offspring. Both had all limbs retracted. Good luck to the lot of them, Lattimore thought, and let's get to hell out of here.

"May you find peace here, my son," said the padre, taking Ainson's hand and jogging it up and down between his own. "Remember that in your year of isolation you will always be in God's presence."

"Good luck in your work, Melmoth," said the adjutant. "We'll be seeing you in a year's time."

"Adios, Sam, and I'm sorry about that black eye l gave you," Quilter said, clapping Ainson on the back.

"Are you sure there's nothing else you need?" asked Mrs. Warhoon.

Responding as adequately as possible to their words, Aylmer turned and hobbled into his new home. They had rigged him ingenious crutches to combat the gravity, but he had yet to get accustomed to them. He went and lay down on his bed, put his hands behind his head, and listened to them departing.

CHAPTER THIRTEEN

THE *Gansas*, or the various men working in teams on it, found many marvellous things. Science had rarely had such a spread.

Before the ship blasted off, the team that worked with Navigator Marcel Gleet finished computations that revealed the extraordinary eccentricity of Pestalozzi's orbit.

Night was a gay affair on Pestalozzi at this period. When the saffron-coloured sun sank towards the western horizon, the lengthening shadows split in twain and a bright yellow star was revealed to the south. This star, though it showed no perceptible disc to the naked eye, shone almost as brightly as a full moon on Earth. And before it in its turn could be carried by the ride of the world below the horizon, another star rose to champion the cause of light. This was a welcome white star that burnt till morning, fading from view only when the saffron sun was again strong enough to take over its recurrent duties.

What Gleet, his comrades, and his computers found was this: that the white, yellow, and saffron suns formed a triple system, and revolved about one another. And once in every so many years, they came close enough to interfere with the orbit of Pestalozzi. Attracted by the mass of the other two suns, the planet would break loose from its sun's attraction and take up an orbit around one of the rivals. When the same juxtaposition occurred again, many years later, the planet would pass to the third sun, and so eventually back to its first partner, like a flirt in an "Excuse me" dance.

The discovery gave cause for wonder as well as mathematics. Among other things, it explained the hardihood of the aliens, for the range of temperatures they would have to withstand, to say nothing of the cataclysmic nature of the upheaval of changing suns, was something that a man could only contemplate with awe.

As Lattimore remarked, this astronomic fact by itself went a long way towards explaining the stolidity of temperament and the imperviousness to pain of the aliens. They had developed under conditions that would have put a check to terrestrial life almost at its inception.

The *Gansas*, continuing its reconnaissance, touched down on fourteen other planets in the six-sun cluster. On four of them, man could live comfortably, and on three of those four ideal conditions were found. These were plainly planets of the greatest potential value to man; they were named (the padre finally swung it on the captain) Genesis, Exodus, and Numbers (since it was conceded that nobody would tolerate a planet called Leviticus).

On these planets, and on four others where the climate or the atmosphere was intolerable to man, the aliens were found. Though their numbers were comparatively few, their toughness was effectively established.

Unhappily, there were incidents. On Genesis, a group of wrinkled-hided aliens were allowed aboard the *Gansas*. At Mrs. Warhoon's insistence, they were taken to the communications deck, and there she attempted to speak to them, partly with sounds and signs, partly with visipictures which Lattimore and Quilter showed upon a screen. She

147

imitated alien sounds, and they imitated her voice. The omens were promising, when by ill luck the aliens captive on the deck below made themselves heard.

What was said could only be imagined, but at once the aliens began determinedly to escape. Quilter bravely tried to get in their way. He was knocked down and received a broken arm for his trouble.

The aliens stuck in the elevator and had to be exterminated. The disappointment at this misadventure was general.

On one of the rougher planets, where it was generally conceded that man would have a thin time surviving, something worse happened.

This planet was named Gansas. It was the last to be visited, and one might have fancied that word of man's coming had preceded him.

In the remote and rocky plateau of the northern hemisphere lived a savage lifeform informally christened a chitin bear. It resembled a small polar bear, but was clad in a pelt of alternating bands of chitin and long white hair. It was fleet of foot, sharp of fang, and ill-natured. Though its natural prey was the small horned whale of the temperate Gansas seas, it was partial to the sexiped aliens that had invaded its home.

No doubt this opposition, not encountered elsewhere in the family of planets, had encouraged a little pugnacity in the aliens. At all events, the first group of terrestrials to fire on a band of investigating aliens was met with answering fire. The *Gansas*, all unprepared, found itself under bombardment from a fortified position set in a cliff.

A direct hit was sustained in one of the open personnel hatches before the enemy was obliterated.

It took five days of all-watch shift work on the part of Engineering to repair the obvious damage, and then a further week of patient and laborious inspection and patching to ensure that all the plates of the hull were unharmed by the shock.

By the end of that time, Mrs. Warhoon had cheered enormously.

"Whatever it was I thought I saw when I ran into that statue must have been a kind of brainstorm," she said, cuddling against Bryant Lattimore's knees. "You know, I was all overwrought that day. I really felt – oh, I had the queerest feeling that man had taken the wrong turning somewhere along the evolutionary line or something."

"Never disregard your first impressions," Lattimore advised her. He could afford a joke, now that she had adjusted.

"Once we get these aliens back to Earth and teach them English, I won't feel so bad. I take my profession too seriously; it's a sign of immaturity, I suppose. But we shall have so much knowledge to exchange.... Oh, Bryant ... I talk too much, don't I?"

"I love to hear you."

"It's so cosy here on this rug." Luxuriously she felt the rug, luxuriously let her finger-tips trail over the alternating bands of fur and chitin.

Lattimore watched her with a detached greed. She had pretty and dextrous fingers. He said, "We hit vacuum tomorrow for Earth. I don't wish to lose sight of you when we get back, Hilary. Do you mind telling me just how emotionally involved you are with Sir Mihaly Pasztor?"

She looked uncomfortable; perhaps she was just trying to blush; but before she could reply, there was a rap on Lattimore's door and Quilter entered, carrying Lattimore's 0.5 rifle. He nodded in friendly fashion as Mrs. Warhoon rose from the chitin rug and adjusted her shoulder strap.

"She's all cleaned and ready for the next spot of action," he said, laying the rifle on the table, though his gaze rested on Mrs. Warhoon. "Talking of action, there's going to be trouble down on the men's decks unless something's done soon."

"What sort of trouble?" Lattimore asked lazily, putting on his spectacles and offering them both mescahales.

"Same sort of trouble we had on the *Mariestopes*," Quilter said. "All these rhinomen we got aboard, they make quite a lot of droppings. The men are refusing to clear it away without dirty pay. Guess what really annoyed them is that the food synthesizer on Deck H broke down this morning and they were given real old-fashioned meat-of-animal instead. The slobs of cooks thought nobody would notice, but several of the guys are in Sick Bay right now with cholesterol poisoning."

"What a way to run a ship!" Lattimore exclaimed, not displeased, for the more he heard of other people's deficiencies, the more highly he valued his own efficiency. Mrs. Warhoon, on the other hand, was displeased, chiefly because she resented the easy comradeship that had sprung up between Bryant and Quilter.

"Meat-of-animal is not poisonous," she said. "In the backward parts of Earth it is still eaten regularly." She had not quite enough courage to say how much she had enjoyed it herself, dining in seclusion with Pasztor at his flat.

"Yeah, only we happen to be civilized, not backward," Quilter said, drawing the mescahale dust into his lungs. "That's why the guys are going on strike against having to swab up these droppings."

Mrs. Warhoon saw the sardonic grins on their faces; the same expression sat with some regularity on Mr. Warhoon's face. Like a revelation, she saw how much she hated this simian male superiority; and the memory of that gentle and superb statue on Pestalozzi helped her to hate it.

"You're all the same, you men!" she cried. "You're all cut off from the basic realities of life in a way a woman could never be. For good or ill, we're a species of flesh-

150

eaters, and always have been. Meat-of-animal is not poisonous – if you're sick after eating it, it's your mind that has poisoned you. And all this fear of excreta – can't you see that to these poor unfortunate beings we have captured, their waste products are a sign of fertility, that they ceremonially offer their rejected mineral salts back to their earth when they have done with them? My God, what's so repulsive about that? Is it any more repulsive than the terrestrial religions where living human sacrifices are offered up to various supposed deities? The trouble with our culture is that it is based on a fear of dirt, of poison, of excreta. You think excreta's bad, but it's the fear of it that's bad!"

She threw her mescahale down and ground it underfoot, as if to reject all artificiality. Lattimore raised an eyebrow at her.

"What's got into you, Hilary? Nobody's afraid of the stuff. We're just bored with it. Like you say, it's a waste product. Okay, so waste it; don't go down on your knees to it. No wonder these goddam rhinomen have gotten nowhere if they've oriented their lives round the stuff."

"Besides," Quilter said reasonably, for he was used to the unreasonable outbursts of women, "our guys don't actually object to shovelling the stuff. They just object to shovelling it without dirty pay."

"But you are both of you missing my point entirely," Mrs. Warhoon began with heat, running her pretty and dextrous fingers into her hair.

"That'll do, Hilary," Lattimore said sharply. "Come off this coprophilous kick and pull yourself together."

Next day, the repaired *Gansas* blasted off from this forbidding planet, carrying safely inside it its cargo of living organisms, their hopes, their phobias, their grandeurs and their failings, transpontentially and transcendentally towards the planet Earth.

151

CHAPTER FOURTEEN

OLD Aylmer was partial to his sleep. He strongly resisted Snok Snok Karn's efforts to rouse him until the young utod lifted him up with four legs and shook him gently.

"You must bring yourself to full wakefulness, my dear Manlegs," Snok Snok said. "Fit your crutches on and come to the door."

"My old bones are stiff, Snok Snok. I quite enjoy their stiffness, as long as I'm left horizontal to do so."

"You prepare yourself for the carrion stage of life," the utod said. He had over the years trained himself to talk only through his casspu and oral orifices; in that way, he and Ainson could converse after a fashion. "When you change to carrion, Mother and I will plant you under the ammps, and in your next cycle you shall become an utod."

"Thank you very much, but I'm certain that that wasn't what you woke me for. What's the matter? What's worrying you?"

That was a phrase that in forty years' association with Ainson Snok Snok had never understood. He passed it over.

"Some menlegs are coming here. I saw them bumping on a round-legged four-legs towards our middenstead."

Ainson was buckling on his leg supports.

"Men? I don't believe it, after all these years."

Picking up his crutches, he made his way down the corridor to the front door. On either side of him were doors he had not opened for a long while, doors sealing off rooms containing weapons and ammunition, recording apparatus, and rotted supplies; he heeded this material no more than he did the automatic observation post which had long since wilted, together with its aerial, under the majesty of Dapdrof's storms and gravitational pull.

The grorgs scuttled ahead of Snok Snok and Ainson and plunged on into the middenstead where Quequo gently reclined. Snok Snok and Ainson halted in the doorway, looking out through the wire. A four-wheeled overlander had just drawn up at the gate.

Forty years, Ainson thought, forty years peace and quiet – not all of it so damn welcome either – and they have to come and disturb me now! They might have let me die in peace. I reckon I could have managed that before the next esod, and I've no objection to being buried under the ammp trees.

He whistled his grorg back to him, and stood waiting where he was. Three men jumped from the truck.

As an after-thought, Ainson went back down the corridor, pushed his way into the little armoury, and stood there adjusting his eyes to the light. Dust lay thickly everywhere. He opened a metal box, took a dull-shining rifle from within. But the ammunition, where was that? He looked round at the muddle in disgust, dropped the weapon on to the dirty floor and shuffled back into the corridor. He had picked up too much peace on Dapdrof to go shooting at his age.

One of the men from the four-wheeler was almost at the front door. He had left his two companions at the entrance to the stockade.

Ainson quailed. How did you address your own kind? This particular fellow did not look easy to address. Although he might well be slightly older than Ainson, he

153

had not spent forty years under 3G's. He wore uniform; no doubt service life kept his body healthy, whatever it did to his mind. He wore the well-fed but sanctimonious expression of one who has dined at a bishop's table.

"You are Samuel Melmoth, of the *Gansas*?" the soldier asked. He stood in a neutral pose, legs braced against the gravity blocking the door with his bulk. Ainson gaped at the sight of him; bipeds in clothes looked odd when you were unused to the phenomenon.

"Melmoth?" the soldier repeated.

Ainson had no idea what the fellow meant. Nor could he think of anything that might be regarded as a suitable answer.

"Come, come, you are Melmoth of the *Gansas*, aren't you?"

Again the words just baffled.

"He has made a mistake," Snok Snok suggested, regarding the newcomer closely.

"Can't you keep your specimens in their wallows? You are Melmoth; I begin to recognize you now. Why don't you answer me?"

A tatter of an ancient formula stirred in Ainson's mind. Ammps, but this was agony!

"Looks like rain," he said.

"You *do* talk! I'm afraid that you've had rather a wait for your relief. How are you, Melmoth? You don't remember me, do you?"

Hopelessly, Ainson peered at the military figure before him. He recollected nobody from his life on Earth except his father.

"I'm afraid. . . . It's been so long. . . . I've been alone."

"Forty-one years, by my reckoning. My name's Quilter, Hank Quilter, Captain of the starraider *Hightail*. . . . Quilter. You don't remember me?"

"It's been so long. . . ."

"I gave you a black eye once. It's been on my conscience

all these years. When I was directed to this battle sector, I took the chance to come and see you. I'm happy to find you haven't been harbouring a grudge against me, though it's a blow to a fellow's pride to find they just are forgotten. How's tricks been on Pestalozzi?"

He wanted to be genial to this fellow who seemed to bear him goodwill, but somehow he couldn't get the line of talk sorted out.

"Eh. . . . Pesta. . . . Pesta. . . . I've been stuck here on Dapdrof all these years." Then he thought of something he wanted to say, something that must have worried him for – oh, maybe for ten years, but that was a long way back. He leant against the doorpost, cleared his throat, and asked, "Why didn't they come for me, Captain . . . er, Captain?"

"Captain Quilter. Hank. I really wonder you don't remember me. I remember you clearly, and I've done a helluva lot of things these last. . . . Oh well, that's past history, and what you ask me demands an answer. Mind if I come in?"

"Come in? Oh, you can come in."

Captain Quilter looked over the old cripple's shoulders, sniffed, and shook his head. Plainly the old boy had gone native and had the hogs in with him.

"Perhaps you'd better come on out to the truck. I've got a shot of bourbon there you could probably use."

"Eh, okay. Can Snok Snok and Quequo come along too?"

"For crying sakes! These two boys? They stink. . . . You may be used to it, Melmoth, but I'm not. Let me give you a hand."

Angrily, Ainson brushed the offered arm away. He hobbled forward on his crutches.

"Won't be long, Snok Snok," he said, in the language they had contrived between them. "I've just got to get a little matter sorted out."

With pleasure, he noticed that he was puffing far less than the captain. At the truck they both rested, while the two rankers looked on with furtive interest. Almost apologetically, the captain offered a bottle; when Ainson refused it, the other drank deep. Ainson spent the interval trying to think of something friendly to say.

All he could think of was, "They never came for me, Captain."

"It wasn't anyone's fault, Melmoth. You've been well away from trouble here, believe me. On Earth, there has been a whole packet of woes. I'd better tell you about it.

"Remember the old-type Contained Conflicts they used to have on Charon? Well, there was an Anglo-Brazilian conflict that got out of hand. The Britishers started contravening the laws of warfare as they then were; it was proved that they had smuggled in a Master Explorer, which was a social rank not allowed in the conflicts – in case they took advantage of their expert knowledge to exploit the local terrain, you know – I studied the whole incident in Mil. Hist. school, but you forget the finer details. Anyhow, this explorer fellow, Ainson, was brought back from Charon to Earth for trial, and he was shot, and the Brazilians said he committed suicide, and the Britishers said the Brazilians shot him, and well, the States got involved – turned out an American revolver was found outside the prison, and in no time a war blew up, just like old times."

Old Ainson had come so adrift in this account, he could think of nothing to say. Mention of his own name had befogged him.

"Did you think I'd been shot?" he asked.

Quilter took a drag at his bourbon.

"We didn't know what had happened to you. The International War broke out on Earth in 2037, and we sort of forgot about you. Though there has been a lot of fighting in this sector of space, particularly on Numbers

156

and Genesis. They're practically destroyed. Clementina caught a packet too. You were lucky there were only conventional forces here. Didn't you see anything of the fighting here?"

"Fighting on Dapdrof?"

"Fighting on Pestalozzi."

"No fighting here, I don't know about there."

"You must have escaped it in this hemisphere. The north hemisphere is practically fried, judging by what I saw of it on the way in."

"You never came for me."

"Hell, I'm explaining, aren't I? Have some drink; it'll steady you. Only a very few people knew of you, and I guess most of them are dead now. I stuck my neck out to get to you. Now I've got a ship of my own under my command, I'd be glad to take you home — well, there's only a fragment of Great Britain left, but you'd be welcome in the States. It'd sort of square up that old black eye, eh? What do you say, Melmoth?"

Ainson sucked at the bottle. He could hardly take in the idea of going back to Earth. There would be so much he would miss. But one ought to want to get back home, and there was his duty. ... "That reminds me, Captain. I've got all the tapes and recordings and vocabularies and stuff."

"What stuff's that?"

"Why, now you're forgetting. The stuff I was landed here to get. I have worked out a good bit of the utodian language — the language of these ... these aliens, you know."

Quilter looked very uncomfortable. He wiped his lips with his fist.

"Perhaps we could pick that up some other time."

"What, in another forty years? Oh no, I'm not going back to Earth without that gear, Captain. Why, it's my life work."

"Quite so," said Quilter with a sigh. A life's work, he thought. And how often was a life's work of no value except to the worker. He hadn't the heart to tell this poor old shell that the aliens were practically extinct, eradicated by the hazards of war from all the planets of the Six Star Cluster, except for some dwindling hundreds here on the southern hemisphere of Pestalozzi. It was one of the sad accidents of life.

"We'll take whatever you want to take, Melmoth," he said heavily. He rose and straightened his uniform, beckoning to the two soldiers standing idly near by.

"Bonn, Wilkinson, run the truck up to the door of the shack and get Mr. Melmoth's kit loaded aboard."

It was all happening too fast for Ainson. He felt himself on the verge of tears. Quilter patted his back.

"You'll be okey. There must be a pile of credits waiting somewhere in a bank for you; I'll see you get every cent that's due to you. You'll be glad to get out of this crushing gravity."

Coughing, the old figure stirred his crutches. How could he say farewell to dear old Quequo, who had done so much to teach him some of her wisdom, and Snok Snok. . . . He began to weep.

Quilter tactfully turned his back and surveyed the stiff spring foliage around him.

"It's the unaccustomed drink, Captain Printer," Ainson said in a minute. "Did you tell me England had been destroyed?"

"Now don't start worrying about that, Melmoth. It really is wonderful to be alive on Earth now, and I swear that's true. The life is a bit regimented as yet, but all national differences have been composed, at least for the time being. Everyone is reconstructing like mad – of course the war gave a terrific boost to technology. I wish I was twenty years younger."

"But you said England. . . ."

"They are damming half the North Sea to replace the disintegrated areas with topsoil, and London is going to be rebuilt – on a modest scale of course."

Affectionately, he put an arm round the curved shoulders, thinking what a stretch of history was embraced in that narrow space.

The old boy shook his head with vigour, scattering tears.

"Trouble is, after all these years I'm out of touch. Why, I don't think I'll ever be in contact with anyone properly any more."

Moved, Quilter cleared a lump from his own throat. Forty years! You didn't wonder the old guy felt as he did. How the grokkies would lap up the story!

"Why now, that's a pack of nonsense. You and I have soon got things straight between each other, haven't we, Melmoth?"

"Yes, yes, that certainly is so, Captain Quinto."

At last the military vehicle bumped away from the stockade. Limbs deretracted, the two utods stood on the edge of the middenstead and watched it until it was out of sight. Only then did the younger turn to look at the older. Speech inaccessible to human ears passed between them.

The younger one moved into the deserted building. He examined the armoury. The soldiers had left it untouched, as directed by the one who had spoken about the deaths of so many utods. Satisfied, he turned back and walked without pause through the gate of the stockade. He had remained patiently captive for a small fraction of his life. Now it was time that he thought about freedom.

Time, too, that the rest of his brothers thought about freedom.

NEL BESTSELLERS

NEL P.O. BOX 11, FALMOUTH, TR 10 9EN, CORNWALL

Please send cheque or postal order. Allow 10p to cover postage and packing on one book plus 4p for each additional book.

Name ....

Address ....

....

Title ....